Midnight Tear

(The Tulsa Oklahoma Greenwood District – A Story of Forbidden Affluence)

DR. JEFFREY A. POUNCEY

ISBN: 0615597831
ISBN-13: 9780615597836

DEDICATION

This book is dedicated to the memory of those men, woman and children of the Greenwood District and beyond: those who worked, toiled and always dreamed of a better day ....

To the courageous who read this text, hereby reckon that a complete picture-window view is only possible to he who fully draws the curtains back...

CONTENTS

Appendix

A. Mazumba Genealogy

ACKNOWLEDGMENTS

I would like to gratefully acknowledge my Lord and Savior, Jesus Christ, who promised Abundant and Full LIFE as well as Mrs. Elois Sullivan, Ms. Eunice Harness and Mrs. Janet Ellenberg — my most marvelous readers. To my wife, Brunetta; children, Xavier, Jenesis, Joel and parents, Deloris and John: I am who I am, in part, because of who you have made me ... GOD, LOVE, MARRIAGE, FAMILY.

CHAPTER ONE

Tuesday

May 24th PM

"The Eerie Dream"

"Roo" sat up in his bed as he awoke from a vaguely recalled dream, or was it a nightmare? The seventeen-year-old boy felt drained and tired, even though he had just awakened after nine hours of sleep. Somehow, it seemed that he had just climbed into his lumpy, twin-sized bed. The lean, but muscular boy rubbed his eyes and massaged his head as he paused to recall his midnight dream-venture that had caused him such an abrupt arousal from his sleep. In his rectangular mirror, mounted on the wall before him, he noticed a tear on his cheek. He slowly and tentatively brushed the tear away from his cheek, using the base of his palm, with his fingers extended upward in a motion that, in the mirror, resembled the removing of a veil from the right side of his face.

He paused and then spoke out loud, "Oh, well, it was just a dream." After all, he was preparing for a real honest to goodness venture today, he thought. I'm going on vacation. Just then, a voice interrupted his thought: "Roo, are you awake?" Randolph Jefferson Author immediately called back, "Yes, Ma'am," his baritone voice projected, "I'm awake, I'll be down directly." "Roo," as he was affectionately known since his birth that humid, pre-summer day in 1904, vaulted out of his bed and stretched the muscles of his 6'1" masculine frame — taller, by far, than most of his classmates. Roo was considered a fine young man by all southern standards. His skin was like bronze, some said; the color of a tall glass of lemon, sweet tea. His head was full of jet-black, cotton textured hair. The salient features of his face; prominent, bushy eye brows, long eye lashes and hazel-colored irises prompted many who saw him to take a second look, especially when he flashed that faultless smile — displaying a mouth full of white teeth. However, the most impressionable of Roo's qualities were not physical at all - his intelligence, manners and unusual maturity level. Roo, had just finished the eleventh grade in his town's only high school, Sojourner Truth High School. He was one of the top students in his class — there were only two that ranked above him — Sally Salts and Benjamin Guthers (now, they were smart). He had an uncanny way of being the first to open the door for the teacher; would often appear, seemingly out of clear air, to help tote grocery bags, crates and sacks when needed; and often bowed when addressing his "elders" — he was always responsive to the wisdom and ways of those who were the "life experts" as he would call them. Roo was known for being the one to ask for his opinion on issues of "boy friend-girl friend" relationships; being a peacemaker and the proper way of handling money. Indeed, Roo was keen on his handling of money. He held a savings account at the local bank on Elm Street since he was ten years old. He found that he was often invited into the bank president's office where he would articulately share his dreams and ambitions. Mr. Smithson, a middle

2

aged, rotund White man, with "smiling" eyes, considered Randolph a "remarkable" and "precocious" young gentleman. "Randolph Author, my boy," he would say, "it's quite in-dubious, you have quite an illustrious life ahead of you." Roo was always intrigued with Mr. Smithson's use of words. His words seemed to lift him to a level where the clouds touched the cool, blue skies. Theirs was a dynamic and symbiotic relationship; and highly unusual given that most white men had little to do with young Black boys, especially given Mr. Smithson's status in the community. One of the Black women tellers once exclaimed after one of their closed-door meetings: "Those two always seem taller when they step out of that, there office."

Roo reached for his hand-me-down robe draped over an out of place, wooden chair and pulled it over his youthful but developed arms. In a jiffy, he was down the squeaky stairs and in the large southern kitchen with its large skillets hanging from the ceiling; wall shelves with tightly sealed, ringed tops and swaths of cloth containing jams, vegetables and fruits and the harmonious smell of baked and fried foods. Like an alarm set to mark the beginning of meal time, the tin kettle on the large stove began to whistle with a burst of steam as he entered. "Good morning Mom," Roo exclaimed with a smile. "Are you as excited as I am about my trip to visit Uncle Ben?" Rachel Author — a stately, dignified woman with brown skin and long silky hair worn in a ponytail, which made her look more like Roo's sister than his mother, and wearing a colorful dress with a flower pattern — faced her young son with softly clinched hands on her hips and replied: "I'm glad you're going to visit your uncle, aunt, and cousins in Oklahoma, but I'll be more excited when you return. Roo, you're a very important part of this family, and anytime you're gone, your absence is felt." You've been such a help to your dad and me; even April looks up to you, even though she's your older sister." Rachel Author, the daughter of a veteran train porter for the

3

"Atlantic Coast Line" Railroads and a home-based seamstress, was a 1901 Spellman Seminary graduate; the first class there to receive college degrees. She was a popular history teacher at the local high school — the school Randolph attended. Mrs. Author would often tell the story of Spellman; always sure not to leave out the part that the school was named for the wife of the college's benefactor, John D. Rockefeller. Roo remembered how Mom would elaborate, in great detail, on the person of John D. Rockefeller, the oil tycoon. She would tell Roo and April "John Davison Rockefeller was an American industrialist. Rockefeller revolutionized the petroleum industry and defined the structure of modern philanthropy. In 1870, he founded the Standard Oil Company and ran it until he officially retired in 1897. As kerosene and gasoline grew in importance, John Rockefeller's wealth grew, and he became the world's richest man; a billionaire. He's often considered the richest person in history." Rachel Author was the consummate history teacher. She knew her stuff. "Mom," Roo responded, "I'm just going for a visit, I don't plan to stay; even if I did, I would come back to move you with me. I've heard so many exciting things about Tulsa." "Yes, it's a great place for Negroes," his mother interjected. She continued, "There's an entire area were Negroes own all the businesses. Not just a store here and there but whole blocks of stores: flower shops, cleaners, cafes. Imagine; every Negro in the city is rich, wonderfully rich. They don't work for White folks, they work for themselves." Her face became serious while her eyes took on a dreamy, wishful quality. "There, White folks leave the Negroes alone. There, the Negroes are strong, they have a lot of power." Roo responded; "Mom, we have a lot of strong and capable Negroes here in Georgia." "Roo, it's different. They deal with problems differently there. White people can't get away with things there. Now, sit down and grab a bite to eat, I want you to be ready when your dad gets back to take you to the train station." She continued, "He stepped out to take April to pick something up. Your sister plans to go to the station with us."

Finally, Roo sat down to eat the generous portions of bacon, eggs, grits and biscuits. He paused and looked up at his mom who was observing his incredulous expression. "Mom," he uttered, "I had a dream, that wasn't quite clear to me." "What do you mean, not clear, Roo?" Roo started, "Well, I know I had a dream, but I can't remember the content of the dream." He paused, then continued; "I didn't think much about it until you mentioned an entire area where Negroes own all the businesses. Now, I can remember, there was a crowd of Negroes in front of a big window ... their faces are blurry to me as I think about it, but I think that they were all dressed in suits and ties and were the same height; I don't remember seeing any women." Mom asked, "Do you feel that you've had this dream before, a sort of recurring dream?" "Wow, I don't know, but for some reason, it bothers me," Roo said. He was puzzled. It was very unusual for Roo to struggle with his thoughts and ability to convey them. "Go ahead and finish your breakfast, son," his mother instructed. "Yes, Ma'am." Roo quietly continued eating his breakfast with a pensive expression on his face. Somehow, he couldn't readily shake the recently recalled, howbeit, fragmented dream experience from his mind. Only the excitement of his upcoming trip to the great city of Tulsa, Oklahoma could compete with the troubling, blurry content of his dream. Just then, all of his thoughts were dashed as his father and sister opened the screen and paraded through the kitchen carrying an extravagantly wrapped gift and meticulously decorated envelope. April Author, Roo's 19-year-old sister, marched and danced around the table chanting; "Roo, Roo, Roo," as she waved the gift first over her head and then to each side. The ample ribbon on the gift whipped in the air as she moved the flat rectangular package around her head; then she lowered the present around and around her body in a circular motion - now virtually spinning in place. She finally slowed her spinning motion, in an almost choreographed fashion, before gracefully placing it on the table beside Roo's half-emptied dish. They all chuckled as the long ribbon fluttered onto Roo's half-eaten grits. Indeed; she had such a warm, respectful and enduring relationship with her younger brother. They almost seemed to be twins — their bond not having been formed in the womb but in their, often, incessant and voracious brother-sister conversations. April had graduated from the local high school and was currently attending Beauty College — founded and operated by Madam Pearl Diggs, a protégée of Madam C.J. Walker. April had always dreamed of being a student in Madam Digg's Beauty College. "Imagine, being a student of the direct, protégée of Madam Walker, an innovator, inventor, entrepreneur and millionaire," she always declared. During one of their brother-sister talks, April recited an article she had read about Madam Walker: "Madam Walker was an entrepreneur who built her empire developing hair products for Black women. She claims to have built her company on an actual dream where a large Black man appeared to her and gave her a formula for curing baldness. When confronted with the idea that she was trying to conform Black women's hair to that of Whites, she stressed that her products were simply an attempt to help Black women take proper care of their hair and promote its growth." April, a pretty girl with long, mid-back length brown hair; bright hazel eyes and a bright smile to match, had a way with words. Perhaps that's the reason she was selected as her graduating class's valedictorian. The Authors wanted April to attend Spellman College, as it was now known — Mrs. Author's Alma Mater. However, April had a different plan. She always proclaimed, "My plans will place me on a route toward establishing a college; a college akin to Madam Diggs." Then at this point, she would always close her eyes, arch her eye brows while tilting her head up and exclaim; "I will be the founder and president of the Author Beauty Academy." Those who witness April's proclamation would often smile and look at one another with amusement. However, they realized that given her academic prowess, persistence and ambitions, she was well able to accomplish her stated goals. She definitely had a presence. Joseph Author was the patriarch of the family. He was a well-known and well-liked policeman in town. He was a tall man — six feet and three inches — and had strong, chiseled-liked facial features. Joseph Author was physically fit and proud of it. He always enjoyed Rachael's glances at his chest. Oh, and how he enjoyed her soft hands as they caressed his salient and prominent biceps and triceps. Many would comment on how much Roo resembled his father — skin tone, hair, stride and smile. Mr. Author grew up in a close-knit family headed by his father, the son of a slave. Mr. Author's father John Michael Author (Roo's grandfather) had nine siblings, one of which earned a business degree from Morehouse College and moved to Oklahoma to "broaden his scope," his grandfather always said. Roo's dad, Joseph, was an exceptional Negro; not only because he was the only Negro police officer in the entire county, but because, unlike most Negroes, he knew his roots, that is, his family tree all the way back to the "Mother land" — Africa. Remarkably, he could also pinpoint the very country of his ancestry — Nigeria. He was very proud of his heritage and knowledge of it. Mr. Author could be heard telling his audience, that is, anyone willing to listen, when his great-grandfather last felt the African soil on the soles of his feet as he was being corralled onto a slave ship. Mr. Author would say: "The minute 'Mazumba' was captured by the slave-trappers, the transition from independent, powerful and driven man to claimed property, occurred. They seized his spear, a symbol of might and bravery, and forced a pick and shovel in his hands." Before Roo could reach for the gift, Mr. Author handed Roo the decorated envelope with a grin on his face. Roo opened the decorated envelope and was surprised to find a note from his female classmate, Brenda Jenkins. Brenda lived across the street from the Authors. In the letter, Brenda expressed her deep admiration for Roo. Roo read quietly as his family looked on with expressions of amused interest. Brenda was known for her excellent penmanship. The letter was written in cursive, with each letter elegantly angled to the right.

Dear Randolph Author, I heard that you will be leaving Georgia to visit relatives in Oklahoma. I wanted to let you know before you left, how much I really admire and respect you. I know that you have always considered me a neighbor, classmate and friend. But, I have long hoped that you and I could be more than just casual friends. I remember our playing in the yard and all the kids running, jumping and climbing trees. Whenever I hurt my leg or arm, you always stopped to check on me. Your attention always made me forget about my cuts, scrapes and bruises. I don't know if you noticed, but, I always tried to keep up with you....

Roo paused to look back at his observing family. Roo's expression was very clearly interpreted by his family; it said "please allow me a little privacy..." His loved ones all seemed to disassemble in unison. His father headed toward the front sitting room while his mother and April retreated toward the opposite corner of the kitchen. Roo turned back to the letter and picked up where he left off.

Roo, I really like you, and would like to be your special friend. I know that it's not lady-like to share my feelings this way, but every time I see you I have a feeling of warmth, peace, and happiness inside. I have to admit that I even attempt to catch sight of you from my window. Every morning I love to watch you, through your kitchen window. I see you look out at your front yard as if you are inspecting the goings on of nature. I cringe with glee and feel a rush in my body when...

Brenda admitted to seeing him through the kitchen window. She loved watching him engage in a morning stretch which usually exposed his flat belly and "perfect" navel. Roo sank in his seat a bit as he came to the end of her note. Brenda closed by expressing apprehension with regards to his leaving — after all, Negro men in the south had a "habit" of disappearing. Many families were minus a father, brother or uncle. Often, it was an unspoken truth in the community. Negroes would go hunting, to the store, to church and never return. Some, who felt indignation, forthrightly expressed their suspicion of fowl play. They would exclaim: "Negroes are kidnapped and lynched, that's all there is to it...." Brenda knew all to well about the mysterious disappearance of a loved one. Her father, Samuel Jenkins, was a man given to hunting, and fishing. The happy-go-lucky, burly man — known as the hunter with the infectious laugh — left his residence early one Saturday morning. It was an unremarkable start to the day during that summer of 1915. Brenda, 11 years old at the time, her mother, and two younger sisters rose and engaged in their Saturday morning ritual of cleaning the house, watering the lawn and preparing for Mr. Jenkins' return. It wasn't often that Mr. Jenkins would return empty handed. He would be seen carrying white-tail deer, quail, wild turkeys, and rabbit. Mr. Jenkins was known to share his catch of the day with the neighbors. However, on this day Mr. Jenkins didn't return. Nor did he return the next day, or the next week or the next year. Mr. Jenkins never returned. Brenda and her family were crushed. They had spent many years searching for her dad. Roo remembered that period. He would notice Mrs. Jenkins in the window of their front sitting room. Mrs. Jenkins had been a vibrant, energetic and youthful looking lady. She had a personality that many agreed, complemented Mr. Jenkins'. When Mr. Jenkins laughed out loud, sometimes at his own jokes, she would also boisterously laugh. She was his greatest fan and best audience. However, when he went missing, her 35-year-old face and body changed. It appeared that she had aged by 15 years. Roo observed that she sat near the large lamp — the lamp that Mr. Jenkins had actually bought her for her last birthday. She would catch sight of Roo watching and would garner the strength to acknowledge him with a static wave; the sort of hand position that could be used to signal cars to stop. This she did between her incessant glances up and down the road. This she did with the hope of eventually spotting her husband ... her children's father. Their lamp was often the last interior light to go out in the neighborhood. At times, it was never turned off. Mrs. Jenkins would just fall asleep in the window. As days turn into weeks and weeks turned into months, the lamp would go off earlier and earlier. In Roo's mind, the light of the lamp seemed to represent the dimming of her hope for Mr. Jenkins' return. Roo's Granddad John, who was a good friend of Mr. Jenkins, would say, "Sammy's absence is death; death is separation from the ones you love. This sort of death is almost impossible to mourn, for there is no body; without a body, death is hard to reconcile in one's mind." He continued, "With this sort of death, there is no funeral service, gathering or flowers. The family is left with an unbearable void, emptiness, that they can't even begin to fill. Does one remarry ... file a claim for life insurance ... move, to be near relatives? In these parts, a Negro must keep his eye out for more than the wildlife."

As Roo excused himself from the table in an attempt to rush upstairs, Brenda appeared with Mr. Author near her side. "Hello Randolph," she stated in an excited voice. "I know it's early, but I wanted to say good-bye to you in person. I also wanted to bring these to you for your long trip to Tulsa." She handed Roo a lunch basket full of sugar cookies. Roo took the basket with a smile. Although he was not ecstatic, he was gracious. Brenda stood watching Roo with wanting in her eyes. As she wrote in her letter, she wanted to be more than just friends, but friendship was all that was offered this morning.

"Thank you, Brenda, this is very nice. This should last me for my entire journey to Tulsa. Did your mother bake them?" "No," she replied sharply, "I baked them myself; I hope you enjoy them." Realizing that the reality of this moment was not matching up with her vision — that is, Roo grabbing her with his strong and unyielding arms to offer a warm and firm embrace — she advanced and hugged him. Mrs. Author and April, observing the entire exchange, tilted their heads in almost perfect synchrony and smiled. The sight also made Mr. Author grin. Brenda was a very attractive girl. She had always appeared much more mature when compared with her peers; wearing adult-style hair-dos and clothes. Brenda turned many of Roo's classmate's head, but Roo thought that she was always a bit too up front, forward and aggressive for his taste. Roo politely hugged her back with his one free arm and then retreated. "Brenda, I appreciate the cookies and the wonderful send off; you're a good friend. I'd like to bring something back for you from Tulsa. Would you like some Salt Water Taffy?" "Yes, Randolph, that would be great," Brenda replied. Roo quickly announced, "Brenda, family, let me get upstairs to finish getting ready." Roo was cleaver and knew when and how to use finesse to his advantage. He knew that including Brenda with his family as he excused himself would save her feelings. Roo's parents watched the drama play out before their eyes; acutely aware of their son's maturity and fine character. Indeed, he knew how to handle himself. His dad always told him, "If you find yourself in a situation, think fast and find at least two ways out." He certainly did a masterful job with Brenda. For now, he averted an undesired relationship with Brenda, but saved a friendship.

Roo darted up the flight of stairs and returned fifteen minutes later dressed in his Sunday "go-to-meeting" suit; a tweed short length jacket, white shirt, bow tie and his size-twelve, two-toned, patent-leather shoes. He held his brass-handle leather suitcase in one hand and his flat-cap, which he wore everywhere, in his other. Of course, while outdoors, it would cover his neatly combed hair, which was carefully parted down the middle. He was finally ready for his venture, no, his great adventure to Tulsa.

After a few minutes Roo's family was properly dressed and ready for their road trip to the train station. This was a family outing, one they had been looking forward to for a long time. The train station was in the next town — an hour away. Mrs. Author was dressed in her ankle-length, crepe flapper, flower-patterned dress. She also found this the perfect time to don her green Cloche hat and T-strapped heels. Mrs. Author directed Roo's attention to the gift left on the table where April had dramatically and gracefully placed it. Roo turned toward the table and paused as he noticed that the long ribbon tied around the gift had remnants of dried grits on it. Roo smiled. Roo rested his suitcase on the kitchen chair and his flat cap on the table. He then reached for the gift. Roo handled the gift delicately as though carrying a small, fragile creature. He turned the gift side ways and then long ways. Finally, he dispensed with the methodical examination and began ripping the wrapping off what appeared to be a book. It was a journal. "Wow," Roo exclaimed, "a journal, what a great gift." Mr. Author and April observed Roo's excitement as Mrs. Author offered, "Roo, a journal can be very important and valuable. The information you write in it will represent your life's journey, your story, your history ... your children's legacy." She continued, "One's history can help to prepare those who follow for their own life stories." Indeed, Roo thought, as he had many time before, Mom is a true history instructor. She never seemed to miss an opportunity to teach, study or record what she considered to be history in the making — no doubt, Mrs. Author had her own journal or diary somewhere nearby and available for a new entry. Roo finally responded, "Yes, Ma'am, thank you for the journal." Roo began to admire the leather journal using the same method of handling as before he unwrapped it. His thick eyebrows suddenly arched high on his forehead as he noticed the stitched initials — R.J.A. "Wow, my initials!" He immediately kissed his smiling mother on the cheek. Roo again took time to admire the journal. He tucked it under his arm, picked up his suit case and hat then followed his mother and April out the kitchen door. Mr. Author closed the door behind them.

Mrs. Author sat in the front seat of their automobile, a black, 1915 Ford Model T, next to her husband. April sat behind Mrs. Author and Roo sat behind his father; his knees pressed into the back of the front sit. Before his father could put the car in gear, Roo was already writing an entry into his new journal. Mrs. Author looked back at Roo and smiled. She couldn't help asking, "Roo, are you already making an entry into your journal? We haven't even left the house yet ..." April who was sitting beside her brother was intrigued and craned her neck to see what he was writing. Roo paused to look up at his mother and responded, "Yes, Ma'am, I was able to pickup a train schedule, a map and a book about locomotives. I wanted to find out the distance between Georgia and Oklahoma and the average speed of the train. I also wanted to know the number of stops as well as the length of the stops. The distance is roughly eight hundred miles. Locomotives travel an average of seventy miles per hour. This will require eleven and a half hours travel time." His dad smiled. Roo continued, "With ten stops, the trip should take 18 to 20 hours — total. Mrs. Author, kidding with her son, said, "Are you using the pages of your journal as scratch paper for your calculations?" Roo responded with a serious tone, not realizing his mother's levity: "No ma'am, I'm writing the information down in my book in the form of a story." He continued, "I'll want my children to know that I am a numbers man...." Mrs. Author couldn't help but laugh. She responded, "history with a numeric flair." Mr. Author interjected, "Son, you are definitely 'Tulsa material.' " This was a reference that was used frequently in the household. Mr. Author inherited the phrase from his family who applied it to any Negro who had "smarts" and "potential.." This, they said, was a person who could be successful in the Greenwood District of Tulsa — "the land of Negro success and wealth." "Listen to what I have so far," Roo said with a baritone voice that almost matched his father's:

> I've just started my journey to Tulsa "the land of Negro success and wealth." I will soon have the opportunity to see the "material" that make Uncle Benjamin and the other Negroes in their community so successful. Although my dad calls me "Tulsa material," it's difficult for me to see. As I write, I am in my family's Ford Model T heading to the train station which is located an hour away. I'm looking forward to the long train ride. Indeed, it will be long....

Roo continued reading his journal entry reporting his travel time calculations. In the brief time that he had made his entry, he expressed great expectation and anticipation in going to visit his relatives in the thriving community of Tulsa. However, he ended his first entry on a somber note:

> While I look forward to the journey and adventure before me, I can't but help lament those I leave behind, my family: my dad, mom, and April. These three have helped to make me who I have become, so far, and I find it hard to

imagine moving forward without their watchful eyes and helpful words. Maybe this marks my true journey toward manhood....

His family sat on the car's stiff leather seats in silence. Besides Mr. Author's handling of the steering wheel and gas pedal, they all sat motionless. This was their first time hearing Roo's thoughts about their importance in his life. It was an unspoken consensus; there was definitely great power in the written word. Especially when read by the one through whose heart it is generated. This was a salient and profound chapter in Roo's story. For now, Roo put his pen away and stared out the window. They traveled a few miles in silence before any words were spoken.

As the family's Ford Model T reached the edge of town en-route to the train station, they were alerted to a curious event, pointed out by April. "Look, there's something going on at the NAACP office." Roo and his family noticed a small crowd of black men gathered at the entrance of the local NAACP office. Mr. Author, down-shifted and slowed the vehicle to get a better look. Some men in the crowd had expressions of dismay; others, disgust and anger. April recognized one of the men in the crowd and exclaimed, "There's Mr. Williams; I hope he's okay." Mr. Williams, a tall, thin, dark-skin, elderly man who operated a shoe shine in the area, appeared to have tears on his cheek. Roo thought, is this De ja vu? He spoke out loud before he knew it. "I know I've seen this before — but how?" The scene swallowed Roo like a gapping sink-hole. Roo was suddenly reflecting on his midnight dream. He didn't even hear his parent's comments about the activities in front of the office. He was again reviewing the scant memory of his dream. He vaguely recalled seeing well-dressed men with tears in their eyes. Some of the men in his dream were looking up ward, as toward heaven; as though they longed to communicate, talk, interact ... some of the men appeared to look down toward their feet, reaching toward the ground, as though attempting to lift something. The walls of the building seemed to be made of brick but, yet, not quite solid. The walls seemed to be behind a blurry midst; no, a wavy glaze, like viewing a background through the rays of heat generated by the hot asphalt in the Georgia summer sun. Finally, Roo's thoughts released him and ushered him back to his family in the automobile. The Authors all knew that activity like this, in front of the NAACP office, meant that there was a major problem in the community — typically an injustice against a Negro. Oh no, Roo thought, a lynching....

Roo pulled his pen and journal out and begin writing as Mr. Author stopped the Model T in front of the NAACP office to investigate. Mr. Author was a policeman in the community and felt that he needed to know the purpose of the gathering — however, he also had a general curiosity as a Negro citizen; after all, it was the NAACP office. Some of the men, after spotting Mr. Author, approached the car before he could walk around to the sidewalk. He respectfully corralled them away from the car and back near the front door of the office. From the car, the Author family noticed Mr. Williams' hand gestures as he appeared to explain the situation to Mr. Author. Mr. Williams moved his arms and body like a leaf-sparse tree, bowing and waving in the gusts of storm forced winds.... The crowd became very animated as they seemed to look to Mr. Author for guidance and direction. As Mr. Author spoke to the men, they seemed to calm down and listen intently and patiently. Now doubled over, as though suffering from stomach cramps, Mr. Williams could be heard exclaiming; "I'll do it, but my heart ain't in it!" When Mr. Author had completed his comments, the men looked at one another nodding their heads and then took turns shaking the elder Author's hand. Before returning to the car, Mr. Author entered the NAACP office but came out within five minutes. It seemed that Mrs. Author and April held their breath as Mr. Author climbed into the car. They exhaled simultaneously in the form of an audible sigh when Mr. Author confirmed that another lynching had indeed taken place. Mr. Author reported, "They found a man hanging in a tree in the woods near the edge of town." The body was mutilated and burned beyond recognition. The NAACP officials are attempting to determine if there is a connection with any known missing men." Mr. Author, now, in an attempt to limit the information he shared with the family, felt he had to explain Mr. Williams' passionate sidewalk display. "The NAACP informed me that they had recovered a few articles of clothing, including a half scorched shoe. As the local shoe shine man, Mr. Williams would be called on in an attempt to identify it.... I'll plan to stop by when we return to town." Roo always felt a connection to any Negro that fell victim to racism, discrimination, prejudice; violence. The looming thought was always — it could have been me or dad; as targets, we all look the same to them. Roo pressed down hard on his note paper as he wrote:

> Lynching, actually always reaches the target audience, that is, every Negro man and woman. It's a message of power; social order. A Negro must always know his place. That place is always subservient and inferior to the one that has the power to take your "dignity," your mind and body....

Then Roo stopped and thought about Mr. Jenkins. Could this have been his fate? With intense pensiveness, Roo's thick eye brows furrowed, as he thought, why don't we Negroes retaliate? Their township consisted of nearly 1,000 Negroes. Whites were only typically visible at some of the local businesses. White mobs usually didn't confront Black crowds. No, they would flush a single Negro man out, like a predatory pack of animals in the wild that attempt to separate one antelope from the herd — then attack. Roo's last thoughts slipped out to the surprise of his quiet family.... "Intimidation is powerful: it always starts off by working on one's mind ... it can make a crowd stand still." April asked, "Where did that come from?" Roo responded, "I was just thinking and writing." Roo poured himself into his journal with the intention of recording everything that he had just witnessed. The next time Roo looked up their car was in front of the train station. With a voice that gave evidence of an attempt to sound cheery and light-hearted, Mr. Author announced, "all aboard."

Things seemed to happen at lightening speed. Before he realized it, Roo was seated near the door of the Negro passenger car waving to his family. The train began to creep forward. April surprised Roo by displaying a sign she had cleverly concealed in the automobile, it read: LOVE YOU BRO. SEE YOU SOON. Dad helped her hold it. His mother blew him a kiss and tilted her head to the side with a smile of contentment. Mrs. Author never revealed to any member of her family that she felt a sense of comfort with Roo's trip. She believed that Roo would be safer, as a Negro male, in Tulsa, Oklahoma.

Once the train cleared the station, Roo glanced forward and noticed the "Whites Only" passenger car. While it was clear that Negroes were restricted from sitting in their car, Negroes were allowed to stare into the "White" car — from their own designated car. As the train's speed stabilized, Roo periodically peered into the "Whites Only" car. In the back of his mind he calculated that they would be in west Georgia in three hours. Roo dozed off to the sound of the now rapid, wheel to rail noise: click-click, click-click, click-click, click-click....

CHAPTER TWO

Wednesday

May 25th

"The Journey across the Great Divide"

Roo emerged from a deep and restful nap like moving toward the mouth of a long and dark cave. He could hear music in the distance. It seemed to echo off the walls of the cave. From where was it originating? Who was playing the music? It was great. The closer he drew to the opening of the cave, the louder and clearer the music became. He felt as though he was being drawn toward a celebration of some sort. As Roo finally emerged from his sleep "consciousness," he was in the middle of a host of smiling and jubilant Negroes clapping and singing. Negro passengers from an adjacent car joined the riders in Roo's car and began singing and swaying to the music. A traveling jazz band consisting of a guitarist, saxophonist; trumpet, trombone and bass players, accompanied a young glamorous looking woman as she sang "St. Louis Blues." Roo immediately noticed that two young ladies had wedged themselves on either side of him — smiling. The girl to his left, seated half on his lap and against the arm-rest near the window said, "Hi, my name's Belle and this is June," pointing to the female on Roo's opposite side. The girl touched Roo's knee as she said, "Hey there..." Belle asked, "And what's your name, handsome?" Roo, still clearing his head from his nap, responded, "Randolph." He was a bit uncomfortable with the uninvited nearness of the two women. June interjected, "Randolph, you look cute when you're sleep; you look even better to me awake." Roo responded with only a coy smile and quickly asked, "Where did you come from? I didn't see you earlier?" Belle said, "We were in the next car," pointing with her left thumb over her right shoulder — her crossed leg bounced back and forth exposing her fancy high-heel shoes. "The jazz band started playing and led us in a march into your car. This is the life; this is what I enjoy about riding on the train..." Passengers were standing throughout the car singing and swaying. On occasion, the train would unexpectedly lurch to one side and cause the jubilant passengers to bump into one another. For many, that was part of the fun. Quickly, Roo's olfactory sense took over. He smelled the not-so-odd combination of fried chicken and catfish. Before he knew it, someone handed him a piece of chicken wrapped in 'light' bread. Roo thought, wow, this smells great. His mind quickly shifted to his journal — he had to record this experience, it was great. He soon persuaded himself to wait until later — besides the chicken grease from his fingers would ruin the paper. Belle abruptly and unexpectedly laid her head on Roo's shoulder. Roo now detected her sweet-smelling perfume over the potent chicken and fish aroma. Roo began to enjoy the attention from the young ladies as well as the altruistic passenger who provided him and his new acquaintances with chicken sandwiches. Roo felt a little guilty for receiving the food without returning the favor. Suddenly he remembered something he could share. He looked down at Belle, who by this time appeared to be very comfortable leaning against him and said, "Belle," he paused and cleared his throat, "excuse me, I need to reach up and get something." The ladies shifted and allowed Roo to stand. He opened his suit case and pulled the cookies Brenda had baked for him out of his suit case. Belle and June both quietly admired Roo's stature and fine physique as he reached over and finally produced a bag. He started by opening the bag and offering cookies to Belle and June. They smiled and simultaneously reached in. He took one and passed the bag to the other passengers. When he turned to take his seat, Belle and June politely shifted to allow him his space. His pants rubbed and dragged against their dresses as he slid into his seat. The movement caused June's dress to pull across her lap exposing her bare, right knee. She didn't immediately adjust it. June was obliged to allow Roo a gander ... after all, she had certainly taken her liberties in staring at him; watching his broad chest rise and fall with every breath — while he slept and now, she noticed his hazel-colored eyes. Roo eventually noticed June's exposed knee; the dark band of her coffee-colored stockings and displayed a sheepish smile. His attention quickly shifted to the inter-car door when Belle alerted them to a curious site. "Hey, look; we have an audience." Many of the White passengers had gathered at the door to take in the activities in the Negro passenger car. It was apparent to some of the Negroes that the White on-lookers wanted to be more than observers — they wanted to participate in the jubilation and food swapping. "They probably wish they were honorary Negroes about now," Belle said. June faced Roo and said, "They always peer into our cars, they're jealous." Roo felt curiously like a fish being admired in a fish bowl. In an instant, a Negro man standing nearest the door, reached over and drew a dark curtain in front of the door. Those who noticed laughed. By this time, the crowd began singing and moving to the tune of "A Good Man Is Hard to Find." Roo thought about the observing White folks in the next car. He shared with June and Belle. "White people operate as members of society. A society is large and often impersonal. Those within the greater society can often function without close and inter-personal interactions. But we Negroes are a community. Communities are small and intimate." June and Belle, still positioned on each side of Roo, leaned forward to look at one another. "Those in a community typically have experiences in common. They tend to share and support one another." Roo continued, looking at Belle, "That's what you enjoy about being on the train; the feeling of community — the singing, talking and sharing... The White folks in the next car don't envy our being Negroes, they envy our interactions as a close-knit community." June mused for a minute at Roo's insight, and then responded, "Where did you come from? Are there any more at home like you? I have sisters..." The young ladies giggled in unison displaying their white teeth and ruby-red lips.

Before the song-fest was completed, the Negro crowd had sampled more fried chicken, catfish and foil-wrapped sweet potatoes. Many of the passengers thanked Roo for the cookies. They complimented him on their taste. Roo had to admit; Brenda did a good job with the cookies — he would plan to share his cookie-taste assessment with her when he returned. A heavy-set, bright-skinned, middle aged woman — she had to be somebody's auntie — handed him a thermos cup full of chilled sweet tea with a hint of lemon. "Thank you, Ma'am," Roo called back to the lady. "You're welcome sugga," she responded. Roo took a long sip and offered June and Belle the cup. They each took a sip while eyeing Roo. They left red lipstick imprints on the cup. June said, "Oops," and used a white handkerchief to wipe it off.

After long, most of the passengers had settled back into their seats. The others returned to the second Negro passenger car. Everyone was full of food, and fun. June and Belle remained behind and spoke with Roo under an over-head reading lamp — the main over-head lights had been turned off for the sleeping passengers. The young ladies briefly shared their journey's starting point as well as their destination — Los Angeles, California. June asked Roo where he was going. Roo said with a great sense of pride, "Tulsa, Oklahoma. I'm going to visit relatives..." Belle asked, "Have you ever been there before? What is it like?" Roo responded, "No, this will be my first visit, but I hear it's a great place for enterprising Negroes." Belle winked at June and said, "Enterprising? Did you hear that June?" "Randolph is not just handsome, he's smart." Belle asked Roo, "What does enterprising mean, exactly?" Feeling a little foolish for using the term with his listeners, he said, "Enterprising means initiating one's imagination, a desire to expand and produce..." June said, "Wow; that sounds like something I'd like to do — expand and produce." When Roo finished sharing the definition, a well-dressed, distinguished looking gentleman with a thin pipe in his mouth and newspaper held between two steady hands with well-manicured finger nails suddenly folded a corner of the paper down and addressed Roo. He introduced himself to the three as Dr. Robert Jones, M.D. He said to Roo, "Young man, you're very articulate and quite right. The community of Tulsa, especially the Greenwood District is comprised — that is, made up — of a great many enterprising citizens." June thought; where did he come from, had he been in that seat the entire time? The Doctor continued, "Indeed, the Greenwood District of Tulsa is virtually self-contained. The entire district is owned, operated and maintained by Negroes. I, of course, have a practice on Greenwood Avenue. The community is a conglomerate of success and wealth. There is no place like Tulsa anywhere in the country. The recent event in this car is a demonstration of a self-contained community. The Negro community of the two passenger cars of this train came together and pooled their resources: food, music and conversations, all contributing toward the overall enjoyment of our journey. Our resources went further given that it was restricted to the passengers in the two cars rather than to the total train, passenger count — White and Black." Roo incredulously asked the doctor, "Sir, we've been on the train for four and a half hours so far and, until now, I hadn't noticed you. Did you get on at the last station?" The doctor responded, "No, young man; I've been sitting across from you all along — you just didn't notice me. Obscurity has its place. Son, there is safety in obscurity." Belle, June and Roo looked bewildered. "I am a Negro physician. My professional training is highly valued in our community, but perhaps too valuable from the stand point of others."

Without pausing, or being asked, Dr. Jones began telling the story of Negroes in Oklahoma. "Tulsa beckoned multiple souls in the early 1900's. They came in search of a better life. Most of them traveled from the states in the south where racism was very prevalent, and Oklahoma offered hope and provided all people with a chance to start over. They traveled to Oklahoma by wagons, horses, trains, and even on foot. Many of the Negroes who traveled to Oklahoma had ancestors who could be traced back to Oklahoma. A lot of the settlers were relatives of Negro slaves who traveled on foot with the Five Civilized Tribes along the Trail of Tears. Others were the descendants of runaway slaves who had fled to Indian Territory — present day Oklahoma — in an effort to escape lives of oppression."

Roo, June and Belle listened intently as he shared the epic tale of the highly sought after city of Tusla. "The overwhelming majority of the Negro migrants wound up in what would become the Greenwood District, the main thoroughfare called the 'Negro Wall Street.'" It was immediately apparent to Roo that Dr. Jones had told the story many times before as he seemed to virtually act out each scene with the care and skill of a seasoned thespian — extending his hands over his head and at times across his chest as he firmly grasped his elegant pipe. "As the Greenwood District began to emerge in the early 1900's, rigid segregation held sway. Segregation, ironically, gave rise to a nationally renowned Negro entrepreneurial center. As families arrived and homes sprang up in the Greenwood District, the need for retail and service businesses, schools, and entertainment became pronounced. A class of Negro entrepreneurs rose to the occasion, creating a vibrant, vital, self-contained economy that would become the talk of the nation. The Negro Wall Street, more commonly known as Greenwood Avenue, has it all: nightclubs, hotels, cafes, newspapers, clothiers, movie theaters, doctors' and lawyers' offices, grocery stores, beauty salons, shoeshine shops, and more." Dr. Jones stopped, and in an almost strategic fashion stated, "Son, I'll stop and allow your experiences in Tulsa continue the story..."

It wasn't long before Roo had both his journal and pen in hand, getting in position to expand upon the events of the last few hours. When Dr. Jones had come to the "last scene" of the Tulsa story, June and Belle stood up and took turns hugging Roo. They politely said goodbye to the doctor and thanked him for the history lesson. The young ladies walked down the aisle toward their car. They both audibly agreed that this had to be their best train trip yet.

The long train continued to make its way north-west, just as Roo had supposed. As the train reached the deep-dark reaches of the west Georgian woods, it began to reduce its speed. It wasn't long before the signs of the cultural landscape caught the attention of the train's passengers like a silent picture show without subtitles. Indeed, the scene did not require subtitles; it was well understood by all who saw it. Through the train windows, passengers witnessed a moderate size gathering of men dressed in white sheets facing a large burning cross. Their faces were concealed with pillow cases; however, their torches and riffles were in clear view. From his vantage point in the Negro car, Roo noticed the white passengers gathered at their windows. Many, Roo noticed, had expressions of pleasure and delight on their faces. Who pulled that curtain open, he thought: in a futile attempt to reduce the potency of the outside event. It didn't work. Like the smoke-filled air that seemed to permeate the seals of the train's windows and doors; the power of the gruesome scene outside penetrated the walls of the train and touched its innards. The Negro cars were thick with emotion. Their guts reacted. The fear was palpable. No Negro on that westbound train was exempt from the profound and spirit jarring experience of knowing that they were the collective target... Dr. Jones made an impromptu attempt to distract attention from the troubling scene. He began to share a modified version of the theory of "thermodynamics" with Roo. "Heat always rises — those on top in society always feel the heat and pressure when we Negroes succeed and do well...unfortunately, when they feel the heat and pressure, they lash out verbally and physically. They must stay on top, socially, educationally, politically and economically — at all cost..." Roo impetuously declared, "That doesn't happen in Tulsa! We have lawyers and powerful business men...like my uncle." Dr. Jones asked, "Young man, who is your uncle?" For now, the doctor hooked Roo's attention away from the outside event. Roo proudly responded, "Benjamin Author. Have you heard of him?" "Why yes, I'm very much acquainted with Mr. Author, he's my professional accountant. Your uncle has been attending to my financial affairs for twenty-five years. I have found none better than Mr. Author in the accounting business. He is highly respected in the Greenwood District." Just then, a young boy, noticing the sight of the burning cross and gathering of those in white, perforated linen, exclaimed: "That's stupid, those people are stupid!" His mother responded, in an attempt to seize some level of control and order over the volatile and troubling scene outside the train, "Boy, don't use that language. I brought my lye soap, good for washing out dirty mouths." She abruptly slammed the window blind closed. Dr. Jones stood up and encouraged that all the passengers to follow suit with their window blinds... Roo, who had come to admire and respect the doctor, supported his resolution and stood to help reinforce his directions. His 6'1" frame and "presence" prompted compliance with all but one man who sat motionless staring out the window. He was paralyzed with fear. Dr. Jones was called to his side and proceeded to check his pulse and heart beat. As Roo reached over the man to close his window blind, Dr. Jones requested water for the man and then began snapping his finger in the man's left ear while applying his cold stethoscope diaphragm to his forehead. The man finally responded. He began quickly blinking his eyes. When the man came to himself, he noticed and thanked the Doctor. Everyone in the car watched Dr. Jones with a sense of amazement — almost forgetting the outside activity that caused the man's distress; but, not quite. The scene would be etched in the minds of all those who caught sight of it; forever. Of course, it would also be captured in written form in Roo's journal. For now, it seemed the immediate and heightened sense of danger was behind them as the train slowly continued past the troubling scene without incident... As Roo and Dr. Jones walked back to their seats, Roo said, "I wish I could have taken care of business with those people outside!" Dr. Jones responded, "Your services were better employed, here, inside the train. Often, the correction of social ills start within your own community — mind you, this is your community." Dr. Jones continued, "Alas, we face a monumental challenge as Negroes; the challenge of allowing for the healing of old and deep wounds. Just as the wood of that make-shift cross and surrounding trees will be blackened and scorched, so will be the remnants that are our memories around that horrendous scene." The word scorched reverberated in

Roo's mind. He remembered his dad's use of the word to describe the articles of clothing recovered in the lynching case back home.

As the powerful locomotive and trailing cars continued to meander through the deep southern forest, it began to slow, now, to a crawl. Roo thought that it seemed eerily slow; this time. The train, which thirty minutes earlier seemed to be teeming with power and moving with remarkable speed, was now seemingly dragging along this remote course of track. It was almost like the movement of a sluggish body in a nightmarish scene. Roo could hear a passenger behind him stop and ask one of the porters about the slower speed of the train... The employee responded, "Madame, don't worry, the train always slows down in this area. There are a lot of branches, bushes and other things that sometimes fall on the tracks ahead and cause problems for the engine. This is a hard to reach area for maintenance crews..." The porter reassured the passenger before stepping away: "Don't worry." Roo considered the statement made by the train employee, then felt that he could understand the passenger's immediate concern: he himself felt a sense of ominous tension, especially as he recalled seeing a couple of tattered, makeshift signs near the track identifying the territory they were transecting as "Klu Klux Klan land." One said, "THIS IS KKK LAND"; another, "NIGGER BEWARE — THE KKK IS WATCHIN." As the train proceeded, Roo could hear the sound of scratching and rubbing on the sides and top of the cars as the uncut branches outside came in contact with the car's metal exterior. While annoying, especially in combination with the piercing squeal of the rail-wheels on the tracks, the sound provided Roo with a minor sense of relief — it gave credibility to the porter's earlier report to the nervous passenger. While this served to settle Roo's concerns, the incessant scratching and rubbing noise stirred a deep level of fear in the other Negro passengers. Outside the windows were a myriad of leaves, branches and dark, animated shadows. There was the sound of the locomotive blaring horn — which made some of the people in the car cringe. One woman could be heard to cry out: "Oh me!" Now the train seemed to drag painfully slow along the tracks. Was this normal, Roo thought. The concern was readily visible on the faces of many of the Negro passengers. The fear seemed to rise up from their bellies... Their faces read: THE KLU KLUX KLAN IS NEAR; THEY'RE WATCHING; THEY'RE BEHIND THIS... THEY'VE BLOCKED THE TRACKS! Just then, across the aisle, a woman with a straw hat cocked on her head screamed out in shock and horror as she pointed to her window; then fell back, hard against her seat. Roo had heard the tremendous thump against her window but didn't notice the source of the thump until it was visible outside the next passenger's window. It was a mannequin painted black. The mannequin bobbled and bumped against the succeeding windows, startling many of the passengers. They noticed the details of the mannequin's face. It had markings that appeared to simulate bloody stab wounds on the cheek and forehead. There were two large X's painted over the eyes, as if to represent death. Before their car cleared the man-sized replica, they noticed a thick rope around the neck. There were screams throughout the car, and children could be heard crying. Dr. Jones at this point stood and attempted to shush and calm the crowd. The pace of the train had allowed the passengers to get a good look at the gruesome sight — swinging and knocking up against each window. Were "they" right outside the train — right now? Suddenly, they all heard a loud thump above their heads — it sounded heavy... Now, they could hear what sounded like foot steps on the roof of their car. This was too fantastic to believe. How could a person actually be on the top of a moving train? However, this could have been very possible, given the train's slow movement. Everyone peered up toward the ceiling, wide-eyed. Then the walking sound stopped. Roo noticed that the inter-car door curtain of the

Whites-only car was curiously drawn. What was going on in there, he thought. He looked cautiously at Dr. Jones who looked incredulous and said, "Don't worry son, don't let the tension get at you..." At once, someone near the door hollered. The excited man exclaimed: "I just saw a KKK peaking through that curtain..." He pointed and finished, "I know I did; I know I did!" A few men stood up as though preparing for battle. Dr. Jones again stood up and addressed the passengers in an attempt to advert mass hysteria. "Brothers, sisters," he said, "please calm down. This is a strange situation, but we'll all be okay. Remember, we're a community — a strong and unified community." Before he could finish his statement, the car's lights begin to dim and the train came to a screeching and sudden stop. Even with the slow pace of the train, the sudden stop caused everyone to lurch forward. Roo was able to quickly reach out and steady the good Doctor, before he fell back. Now, they could here more movement on the roof of the train. Now, Roo knew something was up. He looked at Dr. Jones with a look of concern. At this point, the Doctor also appeared to be concerned. A Negro porter ran into the car and instructed: Sirs, ma'ams; please take your seats, right away. Roo noticed that a few women had tears in their eyes. They heard an announcement come over the public address speaker. The conductor cleared his voice: "Um, Um; this is the conductor... We are experiencing problems outside the train... please sit quietly in your seats and wait for further instructions.

The inter-car doors suddenly and abruptly opened and ten Negro porters rushed in and through the car toward the second Negro car. The last porter looked as though he had seen a ghost — he kept looking back over his shoulder at a, for now, invisible pursuer. They all hurried away from the Whites-only car as though fleeing something or someone extremely dangerous...near chaos broke out...the train now began to budge, *but in reverse*. "My lamb!" someone shouted. The train moved far enough in reverse to bring the scary mannequin back into sight. It was as though something big and powerful was pulling the train backward — back toward dangerous territory... The now stilled mannequin, with the back of its head resting on the outer window near a large Black woman, reminded everyone *where* they were, *who* they were and *who* might burst through the doors the porters had hastily come through. The stationary train made them all a vulnerable target. It seemed that everyone held their collective breath waiting for the porter's pursuers to burst through... 15 seconds, no one came through the doors; 30 seconds, no sign of the pursuers; one full minute, and the doors remained closed. As all observers began to mentally decompress, the door suddenly burst open to everyone's astonishment and surprise...it was the portly, white train conductor heading in the direction of the Negro porters. "Whew," was audibly issued through Roo's lips as he wiped his head with the back of his hand.

Roo could hear barking in the distance. Dr. Jones uttered, "That sounds like blood hounds..." Roo responded with a hushed voice: "What are dogs doing way out here?" For many, that would have been a rhetorical question...of course, the hunter and "the hunted" knew the significance of hound dogs. The question was who are the hunters — THE KLAN, Roo thought. The barking dogs seemed to get closer and closer. They seemed to be on the train's right side. It was hard to see out the window — too many leaves; it was too dark, Roo, thought. The already dimmed lights began to flicker as the train seemed to struggle to move forward. It stopped. Some of the children seemed to find the situation entertaining... "Ma ma, this like Papa Joe's ole 'ruck' " — the little girl tried to say truck. Her mother tapped her knee and whispered, "Quiet, baby." Roo thought of the innocence of childhood, what an advantage. Now the dogs seemed to be near the tracks. Roo could feel the tension rise like a bucket being filled with boiling water. Whoever it was must be standing right outside the train. The train attempted to move again and then shook to a stop. Dr. Jones instructed from his seat, "close your window shades" just as they all began to hear beating and banging on the side of the metal car... "Come out you nigg..." the rest of the word was muffled by the blaring locomotive horn. It seemed that the horn would not stop...it seemed to be a warning to those outside to give way! Some of the Negro passengers ducked their heads in their laps as if attempting to avoid expected gunfire. Roo noticed Dr. Jones reach for his black bag — was he readying his medical instruments in case of an emergency or was he searching for a handy firearm, Roo thought to himself...Roo felt himself preparing for a struggle.

At this point, the lights went off completely. Roo whispered to Dr. Jones: "Dr. Jones, what's going on? Has this ever happened before?" The Dr. winked at Roo and placed his finger in front of his lips as a signal to stop talking. The doctor's wink and signal was invisible in the darkness. Roo instantly thought about June and Bell — were they okay in the next Negro car? Are they crying? What must they be thinking?

After what seemed like hours of incessant banging, the train began to move slowly forward again. The lights were still off. Roo noticed the glow of Dr. Jones' pipe before him. It gave Roo a faint view of the doctor's dignified silhouette — and the identifiable shape of a pistol in his lap. Out of the corner of his eyes, Roo caught a glimpse of what appeared to be a torch outside his window. Was that actually a torch and is it moving along with the train? Soon the lights popped on. Everyone in the car rubbed their eyes in an attempt to adjust to the contrast of bright lights. The "vision" of the torch disappeared as the passenger car became awash in brightness. The now familiar voice came over the public address speaker again. "Passengers, we're moving forward, safe and sound. We ran into a *problem*, but got passed it. We should be reaching normal track speed shortly — thank you."

The train began to accelerate. The increased speed helped to bring welcomed relief to many of the Negro passengers. One woman could be heard to exclaim, "Sooo long, Georgia!" Another woman at the opposite end of the car responded, "Amen sister, amen."

Five minutes later, the train crossed the state line. Only a small posted sign in the thick brush and tree-filled woods marked the point where Georgia became Alabama. Roo sank back in his seat across from Dr. Jones, and for the first time in the last two hours, seemed to relax. Dr. Jones picked up his news paper; gave Roo a stern; assuring look and then went back to reading. Before Roo could rest his eyes, he noticed the back-page story in the Doctor's Atlanta paper — another lynching reported. According to the article, the remains of a man had been discovered on the outskirts of a small township, outside Atlanta proper. The body had been burned and was immediately unidentifiable. The brief notice indicated that a few articles of clothing survived the conflagration and that the local NAACP office had been called upon to help identify the victim. The article closed with: "At press time, there are no other clues in the case." Roo was sure that this was the case that his dad had planned to investigate back at home. In the National News Report section, once Dr. Jones turned the page and adjusted the paper, Roo read the excerpt: "Why should The Birth of a Nation misrepresent us here?" Roo recalled the picture show that denigrated and defamed Negroes. He was 11 at the time. The film told a story of the Civil War and its aftermath, as seen through the eyes of two families: the Stonemans of the North and the Camerons from the South. When the Civil War broke out, the Stonemans cast their lot with the Union, while the Camerons were loyal to Dixie. After the war, Ben Cameron, distressed that his beloved south was now under the rule of Negroes and carpetbaggers, organized several like-minded Southerners into a secret vigilante group called the Ku Klux Klan. When Cameron's beloved younger sister Flora leaped to her death rather than surrender to the lustful advances of renegade slave Gus, the Klan waged war on the new Northern-inspired government and ultimately restored "order" to the South. The film had sparked outrage in Negro communities nationwide. Roo remembered the uproar in his town over the films portrayal of Negroes. It was the topic of conversation in the local barbershop, church, school and, yes, at the Author's breakfast table. The newspaper article reported…when the film was reissued in New York, two Negro ex-servicemen and three Negro women who served in France as canteen workers were arrested for distributing a circular put out by the NAACP called "Stop the KKK Propaganda in New York." The protesters had carried signs reading: "We represented America in France, why should *The Birth of a Nation* misrepresent us here?" They were charged with violating a city ordinance prohibiting the distribution of hand bills, circulars, or other advertising materials. The NAACP appealed the guilty verdict to make it a test case on whether "educational material" could be distributed in public in New York City… Roo felt a high-level of frustration after reading the article. He felt drained; he couldn't move a muscle. Before long, Roo dozed off for a second time on the long train trip. Roo Author was among many in the car that had finally fallen asleep — it was half past three in the morning.

Roo awoke to the sound of the blaring train horn. For the first time in a long time, his sleep was not filled with dream-images. He felt rested. He noticed that Dr. Jones was awake and reading a medical magazine. Roo thought, does he ever sleep? Indeed, Roo thought it hard to even image what the doctor might look like with his eyes closed. He always seemed alert and vigilant. Roo looked out the train window and noticed that the sun was up. It appeared to be a virtually cloudless morning. He pulled his pocket watch out, a gift from his maternal grandfather, and mentally adjusting for the time-zone change, determined that it was a quarter to nine in the morning — it was almost 10:00 o'clock in Georgia. Roo was quite correct in his earlier calculations. He realized that they were now in Arkansas. The speeding locomotive, during his early morning nap, had made four stops and traversed the entire state of Mississippi. "Good morning, young man," Dr. Jones bade. "Good morning, Doctor," Roo responded. Dr. Jones asked, "Did you sleep well?" Roo nodded his head in affirmation and said, "Yes, sir." Roo asked the doctor, "Sir, did you take a nap?" The doctor replied, "No, I'll wait until I reach Tulsa and then slumber." Roo mused for a few minutes, pondering Dr. Jones remarkable stamina. Roo didn't realize that doctors like Dr. Jones spent long stretches of time in hospitals or homes attending to their patients for hours on in — virtually non-stop... "***The shift of a doctor is not measured from sun to sun, but nap to nap***" — was Dr. Jones' core belief. His shifts were the hours between sleep, not night and day... He was use to it. Indeed, Dr. Jones' ability to stay awake was not as amazing as Roo thought. Nevertheless, In Roo's estimation, Dr. Jones was a remarkable and very disciplined gentleman.

It wasn't long before Roo smelled food. Oh; and it smelled so good. His olfactory sense told him that it was the smell of gravy. He was correct. Before his eyes was a platter with the railroad company's emblem on the edge, bearing three biscuits, smothered with ham-gravy, a generous portion of scrambled eggs and a thick slice of sweet ham in the grasp of a gloved-hand. The smiling porter motioned for Roo to accept the food offering. Without hesitation, Roo took the platter and tray. Before he could place the tray on his lap, another Negro porter placed a cloth napkin across his legs. Roo said grace and began to eat. A few minutes later, a third porter offered him a large glass of apple juice which Roo graciously accepted. "Thank you, sir," Roo said. "You're very welcome, young sir," the porter replied. Roo now noticed that Dr. Jones also had a tray. He had a bowl of grits, three slices of bacon, fried eggs, toast and a large cup of black coffee. The aroma of the rich coffee was distinct and powerful.

As Roo ate his breakfast, he looked out his window and saw a curious sight. As far as he could see, he noticed tents and make-shift shelters. He could hardly believe his eyes. He looked across the aisle in an attempt to catch a glimpse through the windows on the opposite side of the car. Indeed, he could see evidence of encampments on the opposite side of the train. It appeared the rails cut right through a very large tent-town; a tent-city. The train horn blew and the locomotive slowed. Roo was astonished. What a sight, he thought. He had never seen so many tents in one place; at one time. He noticed people; White people, walking in narrow lanes between the tents. There were campfires, barrels, cots, wagons, dogs, cats and farm animals; caged in pens. He also saw children and women carrying babies. The people appeared, to Roo, to be in dire-straights. Roo came to consider that in America there existed more than one barrier to one's true freedom, liberty and pursuit of happiness — being a Negro and being poor. Poverty definitely had its limitations and restrictions. Roo whispered; "But, barriers can be destroyed..." Dr. Jones looked up at Roo incredulously, paused, then continued reading and eating his breakfast. Before Roo finished his sumptuous breakfast, which he learned was ordered and purchased by Dr. Jones while he slept, he witnessed additional "tent-city" scenes through his window as the locomotive traveled its predetermined rail-course. Perhaps this gripping scene of poverty represented the proverbial dark cloud with the silver-lining lying beyond: The Greenwood District. He could hardly wait. His excitement seemed to grow as the train rounded every bend. He heard the train's horn blare as the train crossed the Arkansas-Oklahoma state line — car by car. Roo thought; Tulsa, here I come. He set his tray on the seat next to him and reached for his increasingly valuable jewel — his journal. Every new entry added a brick, a stone of information which formed his foundation — his story, his autobiography. Roo quickly became myopic. The world seemed to dim around him as he began to write with great fervor. For Roo, time stood still or did it? He was engrossed, enveloped in his newly established existence where no one could follow unless he gave them permission...the world would have to wait, he had much to deposit; and his pen was the key. The train traveled at seventy miles per hour; Roo's mind seemed to propel him at the "speed of light." Two hours later, Roo's lightening speed thoughts and the speeding train finally rendezvoused as the conductor walked past him and bellowed the announcement: "Tuuul-sa; Tulsa, Oklahoma in ten minutes...Tulsa passengers, prepare for debarkation!"

CHAPTER THREE

Thursday

*May 26*th

"The City in the Black"

He made it! He was in Tulsa, Oklahoma. He could hardly believe it. He had
bade Dr. Jones farewell and promised to visit his office with his uncle while in
Tulsa — Dr. Jones was delighted with the proposal. The doctor had become
quite fond of Randolph from the first time he overheard his discourse on
"Community" to June and Belle. Roo was now standing in the doorway of
the Negro passenger car with his suitcase and journal in hand. He paused to
survey his first open-air sight of Tulsa. He attempted to absorb everything he
could from this, the last step of the train; the Tulsan sunlight, the heat, and
yes, even the humidity. In his mind he imagined that even the soil and
pavement in Tulsa would be different as compared to Georgia. He thought:
Tulsa soil grows only good things — things that promote success, excellence,
and kindness... Suddenly, from behind came a loud throat clearing prompt,

"Umh, umh, umh, young man; will you please step off the train?" Roo looked back and noticed a line of passengers waiting to disembark as well as the conductor on the top step, displaying a stern expression. The conductor continued for emphasis: "We must stay on schedule..." Roo immediately leaped over the step stool that had been placed near the train's step, to the immaculate looking platform. He looked back at the conductor and presented a smile and head nod. He looked back toward the station and saw a prominent looking man approaching. As the man got closer, Roo noticed that he looked amazingly like his granddad, John Author. With a projective voice, the man called out, "Randolph, is that you?" "Yes, sir; I'm Randolph Author." Before him, stood his grandfather's brother, Benjamin Albert Author. He was the splitting-image of his grandfather. Next to him was his youngest son, Michael Author. Uncle Benjamin was his grandfather's youngest brother — he was 10 years younger than John Author. Actually, Uncle Benjamin was the youngest of all his grandfather's nine siblings. Michael Author was 3 years Roo's senior — he was 20. Roo could see the Author family resemblance. Uncle Ben offered Roo his hand and stated, "Randolph, it's good to see you. You bear a strong likeness to your father." "Yes, sir," Roo responded. After shaking Roo's hand, he turned to the young man standing to his side and said, "Randolph, this is my son; your first cousin — once removed — Michael." Indeed, Uncle Ben was his father's uncle; they spoke the same genealogical language. He and Michael shook hands. Roo and Michael were exactly the same height, had the same skin tone, hair texture, and appeared to have the same mannerisms. They were definitely related. Uncle Ben directed Michael's attention to Roo's suitcase. "Son, take Randolph's suitcase." Michael responded, "Yes, sir," while reaching for the suitcase. They all began walking back toward the station parking lot. As they reached Uncle Benjamin's car, a well-dressed, fine-looking, middle-aged, Negro woman called to his uncle: "Mr. Author, hello,

how are you this afternoon?" "Ah, Mrs. Booker, I'm well, and how are you?"
"Fine, thank you." She said hello to Michael, who offered a partial bow and
then she acknowledged Roo: "Hello young man. Goodness gracious, you're a
handsome gent." Roo, responded, "Thank you, Ma'am." Uncle Ben
introduced Roo to the Negro community's socialite, Mrs. Sophia Booker. She
and her husband, George Booker, owned and operated Greenwood District's
bookstores. Mrs. Booker always took the lead in planning and organizing the
town's scholarship luncheons and social balls. She and her husband were the
epitome of affluence, social grace and community progress. Mrs. Booker took
a special interest in the young people of the Greenwood District. She would
often exclaim, "The young people are the future of 'Greenwood'; they will
someday carry the torch and perpetuate the excellence that is our Greenwood
District." Mrs. Booker had a faultless record. Her programs were always well-
attended and enthusiastically supported by young and old. Many in the
community attributed her wonderful record to the zeal and excitement she
demonstrated in her community efforts. Moreover, they also realized that she
always had a willing and participatory audience who shared her enthusiasm.
That is, "theirs was a community that thrived on its collective successes,
excellence and wellbeing." Like a well-fitting outfit, the Greenwood District
culture was an experience Roo was willing to try on and make his own. At this
juncture, he already felt that he was well suited for "Greenwood"; Tulsa. He
was beginning to feel like "Tulsa Material." This was only the beginning of
Roo's Greenwood District "odyssey."

Michael proudly drove the family car, a 1918, Marmon-34 Touring car. It was
a dark-blue convertible. Uncle Benjamin was seated in the front passenger
seat. Roo noticed that he sat with an almost perfect posture. He sat erect with
his back barely touching the seat. He rested his hands on his knees and

looked forward. Roo also noticed an ornate walking stick resting partly on the automobile floor and the seat between his uncle and Michael. It appeared to be quite a grand looking cane with a bold silver handle and black shaft that tapered toward the base. Roo observed that Uncle Benjamin appeared to be quite agile and mobile — he didn't need a cane as a walking aide. Roo thought, then why does he have the fancy cane? Without turning his head, Uncle Benjamin suddenly asked Roo, who was sitting directly behind Michael: "Randolph, how are your father and mother?" Roo reported that they were getting along well. He added, "Activities in our town are keeping my father especially busy these days." "What sort of activities?" his uncle asked. "Lynching," Roo said in a word. Uncle Benjamin paused and said, "I see..." Uncle Benjamin asked, "And how is my bright and talented niece, April?" Without pausing, Uncle Benjamin continued, "I was very proud of April as she gave her valedictorian address at her commencement. I understand that she aspires to open her own beauty school someday." Roo, instantly recalling Uncle Benjamin's visit - along with many other relatives for April's high school graduation responded, "Yes, sir, she's fine." Uncle Benjamin quickly responded; "Yes sir-ree, you and your sister are both 'Tulsa Material.' " Michael had a smile on his face. He was proud to be related — they were his cousins. Five intersections later, Michael turned the bulky blue vehicle onto Greenwood Avenue. Uncle Benjamin announced, "This is Greenwood Street for which the community is named. This street and the businesses hereon are considered by many to be the center; the heart of our Negro community."

Michael directed the convertible northward on the avenue. Roo was amazed at the bevy of activity in the district. It seemed that there were hundreds of pedestrians on the streets and sidewalks — Negro woman, children and men. It seemed that the number of people within his view far out numbered the entire population of his town back in Georgia. Although he had been to Atlanta plenty of times, he hadn't experienced a sight quite like this. The city of Tulsa had a population of over 100,000; 10,000 souls resided in the 35-square-block area of Greenwood District. Roo easily calculated the population density to be 286 Negroes for every square "Greenwood" block. Wow, he thought — the streets are so clean.

After carefully passing through six busy intersections of shoppers, business people and street vendors, Michael maneuvered the Marmon parallel to the curb in front of an aesthetically pleasing brick building. The double doors appeared to be constructed of the finest wood and the wide-windows were paneled in mahogany frames. Every window was dressed with a broad, jet-black, parabola shaped awning. Indeed, the building was elegant. This was Uncle Benjamin's office. "Roo, this is where I conduct my financial business," said Uncle Benjamin. "I need to pick up an important item before taking you to the house — I have a gift for your aunt." Once Michael engaged the parking brakes, they all exited the vehicle. Roo stood motionless with one foot propped on the running board of the vehicle. He looked intently in one direction and then the other as he witnessed Negro women, children and men of every height and hue. Not one appeared to be sad or under-trodden. Many people acknowledged Uncle Benjamin and Michael as they passed. The three Author men climbed ten wide steps covered with deep-dark, soft padding. Every step facing the street had an insignia directly in the center. Roo noticed encircled, an italicized capital "A," a bold period, an italicized capital "F," and another period. Roo asked Michael, "What does the "A" and "F" mean?" Michael responded, "Author Financial." Wow, Roo thought. Uncle Benjamin had already reached the landing and opened the unlocked door. Author Financial was still open for business during Uncle Benjamin's brief absence.

Roo paused at the door when he caught sight of the interior. The Author Financial office doors opened to a large, cavernous, but inviting entryway. Roo, visually-spatially determined that the general shape of the room was oval. The entrance served as the receptionist office. The room contained large luxurious furniture and rugs. Positioned in the center of the room, just behind a large rectangular Oriental rug, was what appeared to be an ornate mahogany desk. The desk, itself, was partially concealed behind a four foot high banister. The banister had a ledge: large enough for a hotel, bell-boy type, bell, for use by customers when the receptionist was away from the desk. It also had a sign-in register positioned in the center. This was also the location where Mrs. Sophia Booker was permitted to place her flyers and handbills announcing upcoming community functions.

The bright-skinned woman working behind the desk was Jo Ann Crosby, Michael's fiancée. She welcomed Uncle Benjamin with a bright smile and Michael with a kiss on the cheek. She said, "A little sugga for my sugga..." Uncle Benjamin looked back at the two and cautioned, "No fraternizing..." They both moved their adjacent heads — like rotating cogs — toward Uncle Benjamin and presented innocent smiles. Uncle Benjamin placed the stylish cane, which he carried tucked under his arm, into an umbrella holder and walked out of their sight.

While in the "Author Financial" office, Michael expounded on the city's population and demographics. Roo was impressed; however, as a "numbers man" and frequent visitor with his parents on shopping jaunts, Roo was very much aware that the city of Atlanta, a one and one-half hour drive from their Georgia town, had a population twice that of Tulsa: 200,616. Of that, 62,796 were Negroes. That was nearly six times the Negro population in Tulsa... **But**, Michael wasn't finished. Being the son of a successful finance professional and an upcoming accountant in his own right, he elaborated on the economic make up of the Greenwood District. "Roo, per capita" (Roo had never heard the word, per capita), Michael continued, "the average income of Negroes in our community is far higher than the average income anywhere in the country. The dollar remains in our community for almost 365 days before being spent outside Greenwood. That means that it moves from hand to hand within our district up to 1,000 times. We have a doctor here who earns an average of $500.00 a day." Michael continued, "Roo, in a 36-square-block area, we have over 600 Negro-owned businesses, including 21 restaurants, two movie theaters, as well as my father's business. Imagine, it would take us three weeks — 21 days — to dine at all the restaurants in the community. We're a community in the black," Michael finished. Now, Roo was impressed. For now, he could sit with not knowing the exact meaning of "per capita," but as his teachers emphasized in school, "smart people should never walk away ignorant — ask questions." Indeed, he would ask for the definition later. For now, he just wanted to walk around his uncle's office; and boy was it spiffy...

Michael, recognizing Roo's interest in the office décor, began pointing out its features. Roo's attention focused on the elegant black Crosley candlestick phone — there was a phone in each office: Roo's family home had only one phone. In the main office was a mahogany floor-to-ceiling bookcase, which contained many of Uncle Benjamin's carefully arranged accounting and financial books as well as dictionaries and a current set of encyclopedias. There was a large European-style grandfather clock across from the reception desk — which had Roman numerals and produced a loud chime every quarter hour. The grand clock produced an almost hypnotic "tick-tock," "tick-tock," "tick-tock." Roo thought, everyone seems to be used to hearing that hypnotic ticking sound; or, maybe they're all hypnotized. He smiled with an "esoteric" sense of amusement as he considered; maybe if I snap my finger, they'll wake up... Roo learned that Jo Ann was assigned the task of adjusting the clock's large weights to assure that it always displayed the proper time. Michael stated, "I usually help Jo Ann in adjusting it; my father has the habit of stopping in front of the clock on his way out the office in order to set his pocket watch." Michael also disclosed, "At times dad will pause when working at his desk to count the number of chimes — on the hour." Michael shared that the gold, long-stemmed ceiling lamps were shipped in from New York City. Uncle Benjamin's desk was a prominent, mahogany, executive's desk. It was L-shaped and had corners that looked like the massive, architectural pillars of a museum. The conference room table was made of the same wood material as Uncle Benjamin's desk and could accommodate up to 10 people. Each position had dark-leather, high-backed chairs and desk blotters. The blotters were always set up with Author Financial stationary and pens. Large, bold patterned rugs were cleverly positioned about the office. Roo marveled at a surprising sight in his uncle's office. On the hard wood floor was a ten-foot-long bear rug. Michael indicated that the animal had been presented to his father by a local Negro hunter. Back in the reception area; on the wall, opposite the immaculate clock, was a large portrait of Uncle Benjamin set in his younger days —circa 1900. Finally, Michael pointed out his desk. The desk, which seemed as large as his father's, was positioned behind the receptionist's desk. It was separated from Jo Ann's area by five large floor vases containing large exotic plants. The large plants obscured Michael's desk from the view of patrons entering the front office. Uncle Benjamin was still in a back room that Michael had not included on the office tour. Roo assumed that it was a storage room of some sort. The opened door, which separated the room from the front office, appeared to be made of impressively thick and heavy metal. Uncle Benjamin called out to Michael. "Michael, I'll be finished in 10 minutes; why don't you go across the street and pick up some dessert from Ms. King's establishment? Ask her to put it on my tab..." Michael responded, "Yes, sir," and motioned for his fiancée and Roo to head for the door. As they faced the door, for the first time, Roo noticed an elderly gentlemen sitting in a large high-backed chair; asleep. He was dressed in a grey pin-strip suit and had a derby in his lap. His thumbs seemed to rest gently on the top edges of the brim as his remaining fingers curled under the bottom. He had a neatly trimmed gray moustache and beard, and was sitting with almost perfect posture; similar to Uncle Benjamin's posture in the automobile, earlier. It almost appeared that the man could be playing opossum — ready at any minute to open his eyes and say boo... As Roo paused to look at the man, Jo Ann identified the sleeping elder as Attorney Ernie Stokes, a retired finance lawyer who had regularly served as Uncle Benjamin's legal consultant. These days, he would come to the office out of habit and fall asleep. "He still knows his stuff," Michael interjected. "We usually don't disturb him," Michael continued. "He typically locks up shop...." While Roo proceeded to tip pass the sleeping octogenarian, Michael and his fiancée continued to the doors with the same level of noise and conversation as before. As Michael closed the office door, Roo heard Jo Ann excitingly exclaim from behind, "Your cousin is very handsome." Then, in a joking tone, finished; "I'm going to introduce him to my sister...then we can both marry **Author** men...she'd be a great potential wife for him!" With his right hand grasping his left lapel, Michael bellowed: "I'll be the judge of that...." Roo thought it a strange response, but quickly made light of it. However, still behind Roo, Jo Ann smiled and elbowed Michael realizing the esoteric meaning: Michael was mimicking Attorney Stokes — who would often finish a debate with a booming voice, uncharacteristic of a man his stature: "I'LL BE THE JUDGE OF THAT..."

Michael, Roo and Jo Ann darted down the steps to the popular restaurant across the street. It was owned and operated by Lottie-Mae King. Roo came to learn that along with scrumptious fried fish and golden hush-puppies, "Lottie's" sold the best pies and cakes in Tulsa county. Jo Ann **just had** to have one of Ms. Lottie's egg-custard pies before leaving Greenwood Avenue for the evening.

The restaurant was teeming with activity. Michael, Jo Ann and Roo arrived in the Restaurant just in time to catch the last three stools at the counter. Ms. Lottie acknowledged Michael and Jo Ann as they entered the establishment by smiling and waving a spatula in the air. The restaurant was an elongated room with 25 square tables in the center and large semi-circle booths along the walls. The metal along the table edges seemed to shine and gleam as they reflected the bright lights inside the establishment. It was apparent that Ms. Lottie poured a lot of time into the restaurant's maintenance and up-keep. The floors were checker-board, black and white. The walls were two toned — black on the bottom half and tan on the top: Roo thought that it looked "rich." The walls had pictures of Ms. Lottie's specialty dishes: T-bone steak with scalloped potatoes and turnip greens; red beans over rice with a wedge of sweet cornbread, and another picture displayed roast beef with a mound of mashed potatoes and green beans. Of course, the picture that stood out — given the Christmas decorations that framed it — was a dish with four pieces of catfish, hush puppies, and beans. The breakfast pictures displayed buttermilk biscuits with dark gravy adjacent to a thick slice of ham; with eggs — sunny side up. Another picture showed a stack of hotcakes with buttery-looking syrup flowing down onto a string of link sausages. The strategically hung pictures combined with the aroma of the food cooking in the kitchen made Roo's mouth water. On the wall, near the bell-clanging cash register, was a bulletin board with handwritten and some typed-written letters, from customers complimenting Ms. Lottie and her workers on their "bumper" service, the cleanliness of her establishment, and "scrumptious morsels," one note mentioned.

The restaurant was very busy and was filled to capacity. Roo sat on the counter-seat with his back toward the counter. He was now a spectator. The high stool gave him a nice vantage point. Everyone in the restaurant was very nicely dressed, as though coming in after a Sunday church meeting. Roo's eyes fell on a pretty young lady, who seemed to also notice him. Their eyes met repeatedly as men and women walked between them — Roo being on one side of the restaurant and the young lady on the other. She was dressed in a dark-colored dress with a string of small and delicate looking pearls around her neck. She had long lashes and long, dark hair that flowed from beneath a neat, multicolored hat. Roo found that he was especially taken by her slanted, almost Asian-like eyes. When Roo finally got up the nerve to introduce himself, a man, who appeared to be her father, stood up with his back toward Roo and oblivious to his presence or intentions, beckoned his two daughters and wife to leave — they had just finished and paid for their meal. The father ushered the family to the door while keeping his pretty daughter close. She glanced past her father toward Roo with a dramatic expression of disappointment, but continued with her father, mother and sister without a word. As her family exited the restaurant, a group of four uniformed Negro men, who appeared to be in their 20's, held the door for the family and entered to a rousing applause from the restaurant customers — and Ms. Lottie. The four men had just completed their service in the United States Army. The young soldiers were now World War I veterans. They moved slowly toward the just vacated table as the restaurant patrons took turns hugging the men and shaking their hands. When they finally sat down, they all had broad smiles on their faces: Two years after the great international war, they were finally back home in the Greenwood District...

As time lapsed, more of Ms. Lottie's patrons left their tables to stand near the veterans. The first soldier was heard to say that he was glad to be home and "home-style" cooking. The surrounding crowd laughed, cheered and patted him on the shoulder. The second soldier — whose countenance seemed to change from happiness to mild disgust — said, as though continuing an already started story, "As we left the New York harbor to Europe, I noticed the Statue of Liberty. It was my first time seeing her... I thought, as the ship sailed past the statue, we are sworn defenders and protectors of our country and its constitution but, as a Negro, I don't feel protected..." Everyone stood quietly and attentive as he continued with a tear now welling up in his eye: "For me, the giant statue seemed to have a mocking crown of thorns on her head, a torch held high — reminiscent of White men intent on finding a vulnerable Negro in the woods to destroy; and a firmly held tablet full of hidden truths and broken promises." Roo had a "lump" in his throat as he listened to the young veteran soldier's discourse. He instantly remembered the article in Dr. Jones' newspaper on the train and the words of the protesting WWI veterans in New York City: "We represented America in France, why should *The Birth of a Nation* misrepresent us here..." The crowd was hushed. It seemed that the young soldier had waited for two years for just this moment to share his thoughts. "What irony," a familiar voice lamented. It was Dr.

Jones. Everyone in the restaurant acknowledged the doctor and made way for him. Dr. Jones approached the table and looked at Roo but spoke to the group, "No matter what the venue or geographic locale — Georgia or Greenwood — the story is the same...social discord and racial unrest." Dr. Jones faced the soldiers and said, "Men, thank you for your service to your country and its citizens." Dr. Jones extended his arms at a forty-five-degree angle above his head and motioned toward the customers in an attempt to emphasize that every Negro there was a citizen. He continued, "Your brave and gallant efforts have kept the world at bay...allowing us to continue our domestic, 'intra-national' battle for true liberty and freedom. Your efforts have not been in vain, gentlemen. Your battle abroad just took less time to win.... Now, we need your continued services for *our* battle on the home front." He looked at the crowd and finished: "It *will* be won, if not for we who are here in *our present*, it will be won for our children and grandchildren in their *present*."

When Roo looked back toward Michael and Jo Ann, they signaled to Roo that they had their purchase and were prepared to leave. After a respectful pause, the three said good-bye to Ms. Lottie and Dr. Jones, and passed through the door to the busy sidewalk. Uncle Benjamin was already in the Marmon sitting in the front passenger seat with that same erect posture. He was staring straight ahead, with a pensive expression. He had a large box on his lap and his elegant stick at his side as before. The late afternoon hours were pleasant in Tulsa. With the top still down on the automobile, Michael opened the door for Jo Ann and assisted her into the back seat behind his father. Roo jumped in and sat behind the driver's seat. Michael started the motor, put the automobile in gear, and safely pulled into Greenwood Avenue traffic. Just before passing through the intersection, Michael pointed to the left, toward an office which needed no elaboration — the shingle on the side read "Medical Office of Dr. Robert Jones, M.D. and Dr. Jim Rothman M.D. – General Practice." Roo said, "Ah hah," as though making a crucial discovery. Roo continued, "That's where the good doctor Jones practices..." Uncle Benjamin responded, "Roo, have you met Dr. Jones?" Roo said, "Yes, sir, we traveled on the same train; he sat across from me." "Good man, yes indeed, good man." Uncle Benjamin responded.

As Michael guided the elegant automobile northward along Greenwood Avenue, Roo noticed Christmas decorations that were strung across many of the windows of businesses, restaurants and apartment buildings. Roo asked his relatives: "It's almost June, the beginning of the summer. Why do people in the district still have their Christmas decorations up?" Uncle Benjamin responded, "Roo, indeed, that is a good question; I wish that many other young people would ask..." Then he asked Roo a question: "Roo, what do you think of when you see Christmas ornaments?" At this point of the conversation, Jo Ann sat up and leaned against the back of the front seat behind the senior Author in an attempt to take in the interesting exchange. Roo thought a moment as he spotted more Christmas decorations and finally responded, "Well, sir, I think of Christmas; a time of giving and sharing; a time of expressing respect, love, and joy..." Jo Ann seemed to ponder Roo's reply as she furrowed her eye brows. "That's right my boy," his uncle quickly said. "Well stated. That's the purpose of so many in our district keeping their decorations in place along their windows, doors, and walls — it's a year-long reminder of our desired 'community relationship' ". Roo thought, once again, about his friend Dr. Jones, and asked his uncle, "Uncle Benjamin, I promised Dr. Jones that I would visit him while I was in town; would that be okay?" Benjamin Author now turned to face Roo and replied, "Roo, Dr. Jones is an upstanding man in our community." He continued, "One can never go wrong forging a friendship with Robert Jones — yes, by all means, you can visit Dr. Jones." Jo Ann smiled and sat back in her seat with an expression of emotional fulfillment. Michael caught a glimpse of her expression in the rear-view mirror.

Further down the street, Michael drove in front of the Greenwood District Community Center. It was a prominent looking building with bright red masonry and Art Deco designs on the top. On each side of the doors were announcement boards with posters and bills affixed. A number of men in uniforms were milling around the double-door entrance. Uncle Benjamin was often involved in organizing the military-related events in the district — and he most likely knew about this upcoming event. He had often stated how proud he was of seeing our "faces" in uniform. In front of the building were a group of Negro soldiers dressed in their military dress: The men donned their tan campaign hats, grey tunics, and knee-high beige combat boots. On their shoulders were the Army insignias. Some soldiers had Cook Sergeant insignias while others had Mess Sergeant insignias. A few men had Corporal insignias. Roo thought that with the military men present, the district must be considered a very safe place to live. For him, the soldiers promoted a feeling of security and community-based integrity. Uncle Benjamin finally expressed: "I'm proud of our men in uniform; they project a great sense of dignity and honor. One of the greatest travesties of our times is society's attempt to dismiss our contributions and make our men seem invisible; insignificant. These men are our national guardians. They all participated in a world wide, international conflict — the first such in history and hopefully the last... The passengers in the Marmon-34 touring car all sat quietly. Michael pulled the automobile to the side to allow a better view of the sidewalk activity in front of the community center. Two of the event organizers, Mrs. Oliver and Mr. Potter, spotted Benjamin Author and raced across the street to speak with him. Uncle Benjamin was heard to say, "We expect a nice crowd for the event. Will all the soldiers be ready to march in with the flags at 5:50?" The two coordinators nodded their heads in affirmation. He continued, "We want this to be a grand event for our men in uniform — they deserve this recognition and honor..." He finished by assuring them that he and Aunt Beth would return to the center within thirty minutes — Aunt Beth was to serve as the evening's Mistress of Ceremony. Uncle Benjamin finished as he nodded his head and looked forward. The man and woman stepped back as Michael looked over his shoulder at the passing vehicles, extended his arm and hand to signal his intended maneuver, and finally guided the vehicle back into traffic.

Jo Ann remarked, "I'm looking forward to this program. I remember the parade we had for the soldiers; right down the center of Greenwood Avenue." She recounted how dashing the men looked in their uniforms as they marched down the avenue. Michael grimaced. It was an innocent comment. However, when Jo Ann saw Michael's expression, she began to rub it in. "Those men in their uniforms seem to have broad shoulders and strong legs. They probably *all* developed their physiques during basic training and while running on the battle field. I imagine that there are a lot of Greenwood women that are trying to catch the attention of those men. Many of them are definitely worth the effort..." Michael, who was usually able to sit with a great deal of pressure without reacting, finally had all he could take and spoke out: "Jo Ann, I don't want you to focus so much on those men... the garment doesn't make the man, the man makes the garment...a man's mind and his integrity should be the basis of his worth..." For the first time during Roo's visit, he noticed a smile on Uncle Benjamin's face. Michael was a wonderful son. He was smart, observant, and always demonstrated great respect for everyone he met. Uncle Benjamin had long determined that of his three sons, Michael would most likely take over the financial business; but for now, he seemed to enjoy seeing this wonderful son of his squirm a bit. Roo watched the playful interaction — which was unbeknown to his cousin Michael. When was Jo Ann going to reveal that she was just teasing him? Although Uncle Benjamin and Roo realized the playful situation, it would not be appropriate for them to disclose... Jo Ann started it and she would have to bring it to an end. She was in no rush, she had him hooked — it was a rare catch. Finally, Jo Ann unhooked him and begin sharing her admiration and respect for him. "Honey, you don't have to worry, I snagged you and won't ever, ever, let you go...you're my soldier boy." At that, Michael presented a sheepish smile, and Uncle Benjamin bowed his head with amusement.

They finally reached their destination; the large home of Benjamin Author. By the time they reached the house, Aunt Beth was waiting in their grand front room — dressed perfectly in a long green gown with pearl earrings and an exquisite pearl necklace. When Uncle Benjamin, Jo Ann, and Michael entered the house, Aunt Beth leapt to her feet and asked, "Where's Randolph?" She spotted Roo as he entered the house and exclaimed: "Roo-ster," come and give your Auntie a hug! Child, you are getting better looking and better looking everytime I see you!" Roo blushed and said, "Hi, Aunt Beth — it's good to see you." Aunt Beth was a dynamic and energetic lady at the age of 60. She ranked very highly with the "social elite" in the Greenwood District, but was always down-to-earth. She didn't believe in putting on airs. She had always seemed to be the perfect match for Uncle Benjamin. They balanced one another. The mother of six — three boys and three girls — she was matronly but yet contemporary. Aunt Beth could communicate with anyone. She held to the passage of scripture in the "***Good Book***": Be all things to all people, that is to say: to the lowly, be lowly; and to the ***not*** so lowly, be ***not*** so lowly... She had the passion and compassion to connect with people, wherever and whenever... She was very glad to see Roo. After their exchange, Roo noticed a lady standing in the corner; it was Aunt Beth's sister, Ms. Emily Carter. She was also dressed for the grand event at the community center. For Roo, Ms. Emily was just another auntie, who approached him and gave him a big hug and smile — she smelled of fancy perfume. After, Michael and Jo Ann returned from the kitchen to store the pies picked up from Ms. Lottie's restaurant, they observed Uncle Benjamin present Aunt Beth with the large box that he had placed on his lap in the automobile. She opened the box slowly and looked in with an expression of delight. She pulled out a green, feathered hat, which matched her dress perfectly. It was another one of Uncle Benjamin's "just because" gifts from Ms. Pike's Wigs and Hat Boutique. Aunt Beth hugged and kissed Uncle Benjamin on his cheek. They all smiled at the sight. After Aunt Beth tried the hat on and decided to wear it to the event, Uncle Benjamin, Aunt Emily, and Aunt Beth exited the house and entered the automobile. Uncle Benjamin drove. Michael, Jo Ann, and Roo would walk to the Community Center; it was only a few blocks away from the house.

When Michael, Jo Ann and Roo arrived at the community center, the room was jammed-packed. The ushers had just opened the over-flow area and began guiding people to the extra seats. Although Michael and Jo Ann knew many people in the crowd, Roo also noticed a few people he knew. Dr. Jones was seated in the front row; the gentlemen sitting next to him must have been his colleague, Dr. Rothman. He also caught sight of Mr. Stokes, the elderly attorney who had taken a nap in his uncle's office and, yes, there was Mrs.

Booker, the woman he had met outside the train station — she caught Roo's attention by waving her fancy fan in his direction. The program arranged by Uncle Benjamin and his colleagues flowed well. A couple of poems were read; a local church choir sang two selections, a skit was performed and awards were given out. Before the speaker's presentation, the community band played two selections. The keynote speaker was Lieutenant Scott House, one of a few Negro officers in the Army. Upon his completion, the crowd gave him a standing ovation. Roo hoped that he could remember everything he had seen and heard; he wanted to include the evening's event in his journal — now in his suitcase at his relative's house. He suddenly remembered the printed program in his pocket; this would help him remember all the program participants. As the program drew to an end, the Negro soldiers stood in perfect formation as Aunt Beth and Aunt Emily sang a soul-stirring rendition of "God Bless America." Aunt Beth had an amazing 1st soprano voice. It was perfectly complimented with Aunt Emily's alto voice. The audience joined in and sang in three-part harmony: soprano, alto, and tenor; a few baritone voices could be heard — which turned a few heads in the crowd. Indeed, as many in the audience closed their eyes, it sounded to them as if the entire community of Greenwood sang the resounding last line: "God – Bless – A-mer-i-caaa; My Hommmme – Sweeeeeet – Hommmmmmme."

CHAPTER FOUR

Friday

May 27ᵗʰ

"Don't Cross the Line"

Following thirty minutes of family entertainment — a song from Michael's brother-in-law Lawrence; an amazing and long poem from 9-year-old Lucy Author; a piano piece from cousin Billie; and books of the Bible drill from Lil' Abraham — the entire Tulsa Author family was finally gathered at the voluminous dining room table and said grace. Author family members from around the Greenwood community and beyond were present. Many of Uncle Benjamin's siblings' children had also moved to Tulsa. Roo had cousins galore... The grand table was full of all of Aunt Beth's popular dishes: turkey with dressing, ham, fried chicken, collared greens, sautéed squash, green beans, corn, rice and biscuits... Mid-way through the feast, Aunt Beth smiled at Roo and asked what he thought of Tulsa. Roo, with his hands in his lap and body slightly craned, indicated that he was very impressed with the Greenwood community — from end to end. Roo also expressed his interest in venturing to downtown Tulsa. Uncle Benjamin warned Roo of the risk of "crossing the line" in Tulsa...He indicated that there was an increased presence of the Klu Klux Klan recently. Negroes there suspected that the Klan's appearance was due to their jealousy of the Greenwood District and those who had established it. When Roo heard Uncle Benjamin's warning of the Klu Klux Klan, his heart sank. His mind instantly transported him back to the scene of the Klu Klux Klan gathering in the Georgia woods during his train trip. Uncle Benjamin's voice quickly brought his mind back to the Author's dinning room table. Uncle Ben said, grimly: "If you cross the line, those on the other side are apt to follow you back..." Uncle Ben continued, "Roo, I want you to take in the sights and enjoy yourself. You've worked hard in school and deserve wonderful and exciting ventures; however, you are in my care, and I want you to stay with your cousin Michael when you leave the house." He paused for emphasis. Uncle Ben had the attention of everyone in the room. Among the Tulsa family members, he was considered the patriarch. Uncle Ben was never questioned about his decisions concerning family issues — and there were many of them. Every family member, those of Uncle Ben's immediate family as well as those extended family members, depended upon the wisdom of their elder. His knowledge and voice were rarely ignored and even more rarely, wrong.

"Yes," Uncle Benjamin exclaimed, "things are changing here in Greenwood District. Things are getting better for us. However, our betterment makes us more visible. Indeed, we are being scrutinized by our 'observers.' We have — without our permission; volition — become the social-economic

'thermometers.' We are used to keep track of the overall experience of 'life'...
Indeed, we are a very important people. Life could not proceed without our
likes...we are needed to set the pace, to be the benchmark, to serve as an
indicator of what is good or what is worse. Never, what is okay or
acceptable." Everyone in the dining room quietly listened to Uncle Benjamin,
although they didn't quite understand his analogy. He continued: "But even
inanimate objects, objects that have no breath or life, can become items of ill-
repute and disfavor. A thermometer, for all its utility, can be despised and
have a great amount of disdain directed at it — not for its general and
beneficial utility and function, but for the *value* placed on its information."
He looked at Michael, and then in Roo's direction. "The thermometer will
display the temperature — if extremely hot, the mercury in it will rise to its
extreme point. If the one monitoring its measurement hates and despises the
heat, he might well attack and damage the messenger (the thermometer) to
spite the message (the heat). But," he paused and looked around the room at
his respectfully quiet family, "be assured; the absence of the thermometer
does not do away with the unwanted heat, it only limits one's ability to
measure it or quantify it." Roo considered that Uncle Benjamin could, at this
moment, rival a philosophy professor. Uncle Benjamin put his head down for
a minute. Then, with the intensity of a fruit inspector, he seemed to aptly look
at the youngest to the oldest observers in the room and stated, "You are the
thermometers... You each speak to the quality of the lives of those who
observe you — don't let them break you...don't ever position yourself to be
broken..." Aunt Beth presented her husband with a cool glass of sweet tea
and sat down next to him. This represented the end of Uncle Benjamin's
"sayings"... Everyone smiled and began to disperse into the kitchen and front
room.

While Michael ran to the neighborhood store to pick up some ice cream for the pie, Roo chatted with his cousins while looking out one of the front windows. As he gazed out the window, he noticed a bizarre and peculiar looking tree. It was an inanimate object that reminded him of a person who was quite alive — Mr. Williams, the shoe shine man back home in Georgia. The tree was thin, and lacked an abundance of leaves. The air was still. The tree didn't move. But Roo could remember Mr. Williams' violent and dramatic movement as he spoke to his dad outside the NAACP office. He recalled the state of distress Mr. Williams was in as he, not unlike the leaf-bare tree outside his uncle's window, moved up and down; side to side; backwards and forwards. Here, Roo's imagination made the bare tree outside the window, move... In Georgia, Mr. Williams had seemed to use every ounce of his energy and every inch of his body to report his thoughts concerning the Georgia death. At this point, the scrawny tree "wedged" another opening in his mind. He now had remembered the distress on the faces of the men in his dream at home. Roo was entranced...he didn't even notice or respond to the voices of his relatives in the room sitting behind him, nor did he hear Michael as he entered the house from his jaunt to the market.

Still reflecting on the "dreamscape," the figures in Roo's dream seemed to be extremely distressed and in utter turmoil. It seemed that the well-dressed men had stopped reaching upward and downward. Perhaps they had come to realize their limitations. The situation was beyond their ability to correct or control. Perhaps their energies went toward bemoaning their predicament — the predicament of their loved ones — their great loss despite their best efforts... Roo's mind was now back with his Greenwood relatives as someone called his name. He could now hear the voice of his Aunt Beth, "Roo, Roo" — it almost sounded as though she was singing his name — "come and get your apple pie and vanilla ice cream; hurry in son..." Roo turned away from the window and without noticing that those who were in the room earlier had left him to get their dessert, felt a sense of dread as he walked through the front room toward the dining room. He now sensed that the background buildings in his dream eerily matched the storefronts, windows, and buildings in the Greenwood District. He shuddered. The feeling of dread was palpable for him. But, it was only a dream — wasn't it? He tried to shake it off. Aunt Beth asked, "What's wrong, Roo?" He had now entered the dining room to join the rest of the family. "Nothing, Ma'am," he responded. "I was just daydreaming..."

Reverend Stokley, a minister visiting from Alabama, and having just entered the Author house for a late Friday afternoon fellowship, was sitting at the table. He was a prominent looking gent with a deep-dark moustache and beard — he recently had been the guest speaker at Uncle Benjamin and Aunt Beth's church. In a respectful but projective pose, he responded with a strong southern drawl and in the tone of a sermon: "My lamb, another one... Son," he drew the word out as if preaching, "are you," he said in staccato and paused, "a dreamer," he paused again and then finished, "or, are you, a thinker?" He raised his arms as though signaling that a touch-down had been scored. Uncle Benjamin sat in the background smiling... Roo looked at the preacher and cleared his throat and said, "Sir, I believe that I am becoming both — a dreamer and a thinker. It seems that I dream of things to come, and think a lot about the things that are... sometimes I spend hours thinking of ways of making my dreams more a part of the way things should be." Everyone in the room, even the children, stopped and mused. It was evident to most everyone that Roo was a thinker. It took a thinker to respond the way he did to the preacher. Reverend Stokeley responded, after himself clearing his throat: "What is your name son?" "My name is Randolph Author, sir..." Roo responded, including his last name as his father had taught him to do. " 'Master' Randolph, I think I shall always remember that. With your permission I'd like to share that with my audiences...It ain't no harm dreamin'; specially if we follow it up with good actions." Michael and the other family observers were flabbergasted. Uncle Benjamin placed his thumb under his chin and his index finger, pointing upward over his nose, and continued to grin. He thought, indeed, my nephew is a thinker...a thinker for the ages. Reverend Stokeley was intrigued. " 'Master' Randolph," he again used the word master as Jesus' disciples used it in the Bible — to mean teacher, "can you give me an example of the dreams you would like to see realized?" Roo, now sitting at the table with the adults — an unusual sight — paused and then said, "Why, yes, sir; I would like to see a day where Negroes and Whites begin to see their similarities rather than their differences; and move toward embracing rather than rebuffing one another: that requires less emotional energy as compared to hatred..." The reverend took a handkerchief from his pant pocket and began to wipe his forehead. He looked over at Aunt Beth's sister, Emily, and asked, "Sister, would you mind bringing me another glass of sweet tea?" Jo Ann was tuned in to this conversation, as when she listened in to Roo's conversation with his Uncle Benjamin in the automobile, on the day of his arrival. She was beginning to get a real good sense of who Randolph Author was. He was a smart, observant, and well-spoken young man; destined to greatness, she thought. This is someone I would really like my sister to meet. You can't go wrong with a Author man... Jo Ann then looked at her fiancé, Michael, sitting at her side. She considered that he was extraordinarily handsome, capable and confident. She pondered: I'm glad I have my Author man. Now falling deeper in thought, she laid her head on her fiancé's shoulder and thought about her family. She and her two sisters were taught to understand and value the "story behind the face." The story was one's family values, family history, and family traditions. This, she learned early on, was the material of character. This was the structure of a real man — the skeleton of who a person really is. If a man respects his mother and father, he will most likely respect you; her mother always reminded them. Somewhere in Georgia, she knew that Roo, like her sweetheart Michael, had parents that labored long and hard to produce the "fruit" that was Randolph Author. Of course, Michael's parents, Benjamin and Bethany Author, could have aptly affirmed her deduction about Joseph and Rachel Author — they were the personified stories behind the extraordinary "face" of Roo. Jo Ann resolved that she was going to introduce her sister to Roo — she simply had to sample the "fruit"... she raised her head and looked at Michael with a heart-warming smile. As the women began to collect the dishes and utensils from the table, Jo Ann stood up, pinched Michael's side, and retreated to the kitchen behind Aunt Beth — her soon-to-be mother-in-law.

Upon finishing his dessert, Roo asked Michael, "Michael, can you take me to a shoe-shine; I want to have my shoes shined for the picture show tomorrow." Michael, who had just inserted his last piece of pie and ice cream in his mouth, nodded his head in affirmation. After swallowing, he said, "Yeah brother, I think we can find someone that's still open..." They both excused themselves from the table. They paused as the visiting preacher said, "You young fellows have a good evening." Then he looked at Roo and said, "Son, I look forward to talking with you again — soon..." Roo smiled and said, "Yes, sir..." Uncle Benjamin nodded his head. They took their plates into the kitchen where the women were talking. Michael smiled at his mother and placed his dish in the sink of tepid dish water; Roo followed suit — with a smile that matched Michael's. "Mom — Jo Ann; Roo, and I are going to Greenwood Avenue to get his shoes shined. They both nodded in unison.

Michael and Roo opened and walked past the screen door. It was a lovely evening. Michael reached for the keys to the automobile, but Roo asked, "Michael, is it too far to walk?" Michael responded, "No, bro.; let's do it..." They traversed the large yard to the sidewalk and were on their way to the shoe-shine. Roo quickly looked over at the bizarre tree across the street as they headed to the corner. He thought, boy; that tree gives me the willies...

Michael and Roo walked quietly for the first few minutes, then Michael said, "I'm full; that was a great dinner, wasn't it?" Roo responded, "It sure was...Aunt Beth is a great cook." "Yeah, she is," Michael agreed. Michael added with a smile, "You know, Jo Ann fried the chicken..." "Really?" Roo asked with a voice of surprise. "Yeah," Michael said with a sense of pride. "I'm marrying a great cook. She comes from a line of good cooks: her mother and sisters can cook — and bake..." Roo smiled, silently, while carrying his "Sunday-go-to-meeting" shoes pinched between his fingers and thumb. He and Michael were not interested in getting there fast; they took their time — sometimes stopping as they talked. Michael said, as they stopped in front of Mr. Elmo's Corner store, "Roo, I would like for you to meet Jo Ann's family, especially Jo Ann's youngest sister. She's a real nice girl; I think she's 18 or 19." Roo responded, "Oh, an older woman." He chuckled. Roo continued, "You know that I'm only 17 years old?" Michael laughed at Roo's sarcasm and said, "But you're so mature, bro..." They both chuckled. Roo asked, "Michael, how do you know I don't already have a girlfriend waiting for me back in Georgia?" Michael paused as though struggling over whether or not to respond, then finally said: "We asked April..." This was another opportunity to pause — they were in front of a law office. Roo abruptly shot off: "We? Who are we? And when did you speak to April?" "Don't get upset bro, we didn't mean any harm," Michael assured Roo. "Your parents called before my dad and I left the house to pick you up at the train station. They thought your train had already arrived and you were at the house. April got on the phone to talk to me, and I allowed her to say hello to Jo Ann. Jo Ann had already began asking questions about you before your family called, so she took the opportunity to ask your sister about any girlfriends. Knowing my cousin, April, I don't think she would have revealed that personal information seriously: I think she thought it was amusing and just told Jo Ann what she thought she wanted to hear..." They began walking again. Roo didn't respond to Michael's explanation — he displayed an expression of disappointment. Michael changed the subject. "Roo, I'm impressed with the way you responded to the preacher back at the house..." This comment brought Roo out of his frustration. Michael continued, "Wow, that was some response... I think everyone there was dumbfounded with your comment. Where did that come from?" "Michael," Roo said in a slight state of exasperation as though Michael should already know the answer, "we're Author men. We're observers; we're thinkers; we're debaters..." Michael got it...he knew what Roo said was true. It seemed those were always the characteristics and qualities his dad mentioned when talking about their family history. It almost seemed to be a family slogan or theme. Although it crossed his mind, Michael knew better than repeating the theme of Roo being "so mature" — it might bring their earlier "girlfriend" conversation back to mind, along with sore feelings... he knew to stay away from that topic. He didn't have to bother; they just arrived at the shoe-shine.

There standing in front of them was a tall, thin, middle-aged man — Mr. Washington, the shoe-shine man. His smile displayed four perfectly placed gold teeth, where his top incisors use to be. "Hello, young fellows," he said with a booming, baritone voice. They both responded in unison, "Hello, sir."

Mr. Washington said, "Ah, I see you have a pair of shoes for my care..." He took the shoes from Roo and inspected them; he pinched the shoes together between his thumb and finger and turned them back and forth while rubbing his other thumb across his left cheek — along a long, protruding scar. "My, these are spiffy shoes; they don't need much work. Son, where did you buy these shoes?" "Sir, I'm from Georgia; I bought them there at a local shoe store," Roo explained. "Umm, I might very well ask you to ship me a pair when you get back to Georgia — I wear size 12," Mr. Washington said with an even larger smile. Roo explained, "This is a second pair I brought with me...I'm waiting to wear my **brand new** shoes to church on Sunday." Mr. Washington set the shoes on his stand, looked over at Michael, and shrugged. He responded to Roo while pointing at a wooden chair: "Okay, son, just sit right here and I'll be finished with these fine shoes in ten minutes."

While Mr. Washington worked on Roo's shoes, Michael said, "Roo, come on, let's go across the street to Mr. Button's Produce Market, while Mr. Washington shines your shoes; he has the best cantaloupes..." Mr. Washington looked up from his shoe-shinning task as they dismissed themselves — he had overheard their plan and continued his work on the shoes. As they turned to cross the street, Roo's eyes fell on a pretty, brown-skinned girl dressed in a blue dress on the opposite side. She hadn't yet noticed Michael and Roo; or, at least, she pretended not to notice them. Her hair was straight and long. It was pinned behind her delicate-looking ear lobes — and reached her mid-back. Her beautiful face was fully exposed. She had a slight nose, fine lips, and full cheeks. Her modest attire did little to conceal her wonderful figure — it reminded Roo of his grandfather John's hour-glass. She appeared to be standing in front of the produce market with a younger sibling. Roo noticed that she appeared to focus her full attention on her sister — as with maternal care and diligence. As her young sister appeared to express a desire for something in the beautiful woman's purse, candy perhaps, she began batting her long eye lashes as if mentally processing the little girl's words. Roo whispered to himself, "Boy, she's lovely..." He didn't notice Michael's glance in his direction in reaction to his muffled and unintelligible whisper. It seemed that Roo had a habit of doing that... Roo wanted to get to where she was. All that separated them was the Greenwood Avenue traffic. Once the street was clear of the pesky, passing automobiles and trucks — and after fanning the dark fumes produced by a particularly slow moving truck — Roo and Michael made their way to the other side; toward the gorgeous young lady. It was at this point that the girl glanced up toward the approaching young men. At that moment she smiled, displaying a set of straight, white teeth. Roo and Michael were in the middle of the street when she and her sister finally stepped off the curb to cross in the opposite direction. Boy, Roo thought, I thought she would wait on the sidewalk — I really want to get to know her. The four met in the crosswalk. Roo and the young lady stared at one another as they passed — they said, "Hi" in unison. She had a sweet and calming voice. She looked back over her shoulder briefly at Roo and then focused her attention back on the little girl walking with her. Roo admired the attention she gave her sister. Roo continued to gaze at the young lady and suddenly left Michael's side and darted back toward the young lady and the middle of the street. To his surprise, an unsuspecting motorist slammed on his brakes to avoid hitting him — the large vehicle came within inches of the young man's body. With a cross expression, the driver laid on his loud horn. All Roo could do is stand in front of the hood of the vehicle with a look of surprise and embarrassment. On the one side of the street, Michael stood on the curb, violently shaking his head, while on the opposite side of the street, the young lady stood astonished, with her hand covering her mouth. Roo moved out of the path of the vehicle, toward the curb where the young lady stood. Without the slightest hint of nervousness he called to her: "What's your name?" The young woman collected herself and replied, "Remy." Roo considered the quality of her voice as angelic — maybe the car *had* hit him and he was now communicating with a spiritual being... he could "see" no one but Remy — everyone had now disappeared into a veil of darkness; even Remy's little sister was shrouded in Roo's peripheral darkness — only he and Remy existed in his focal point. "ROO...ROO!" "Ohhh, uhh," he was still in his terrestrial existence as he heard Michael's harsh-sounding voice holler: "BOY!!! Get out of the street and get over here!" Roo came to himself; quickly monitored the traffic, and hurried back across the street toward his cousin. Before he reached the curb, Remy called after him with a delightful tone, "And what's your name?" Roo turned and shouted back, "Randolph Author!" She caught hold of her little sister's hand and before heading off toward a neighboring dress store responded, "You watch yourself now; come and visit me at 'Button's'; my grandfather's store..." Her more intimate thought was: "Take care of that nice body of yours — I'll want to see you again soon." She had hoped that she hadn't sounded too flirtatious — there were a lot of eyes and ears in their vicinity; including those of her grandparents. The *worst anyone* could think about young Ms. Remy was that she was "alluring"; she was much too attractive and well-off to be considered desperate by anyone's measure. Once Roo had come to within arm-length of Michael, Michael — who was about the same size and height as Roo — quickly caught Roo around the neck and placed him in a head-lock. He forced Roo to bend over. Michael then playfully, but firmly, removed Roo's flat-cap and started hitting the top of his head with the cap. Michael hit Roo's head while stating in staccato: "Boy –you – goin' – around – about – to– get – hit – by – a – car – and – get – me – in – trouble." Each word came before a swat to Roo's head. He released Roo who was still doubled over with his hands on his knees. Some of the passers-by watched with amusement.

Roo finally stood up as Michael tossed his cap at him. Roo caught it with one hand. Michael teasingly said, "Now here, you hold my hand..." Roo smiled at Michael, and then turned to look across the street to see if he could catch sight of Remy. No success. Michael demanded, "Com'on." They went inside of Button's Produce, Remy's grandparents' store, to get the cantaloupe. A few minutes later they were leaving the store. As they reached the curb, they saw Mr. Washington waving to them. He called over the traffic noise, "I'm finished with your shoes!" Michael looked at Roo and said, "Let's get your shoes and move on..." Roo asked Michael, "Are you going to tell Uncle Benjamin what happened?" "Are you joshing? No; if I let him know what you did, he would stop us from going to 'town' tomorrow," Michael shot back. When the traffic cleared, Michael cupped the back of Roo's neck like a vise and proceeded to usher him across the street to the shoe-shine shop. Once back in front of the shoe-shine shop, Mr. Washington handed Roo his shoes. Roo inspected his shoes with a smile and gave the shoe-shine man his fee and included a tip. "Thank you, sir," Roo added. "Come back again, and don't forget my 'Georgia shoe' order — size 12," Mr. Washington said with a broad, gleaming smile, while plucking his suspenders with his thumbs...

"Okay," Michael said almost exhausted. It was getting late and many of the stores were closing down. Michael said, "Before we head to the house, I want to show you something." Without questioning Michael's suggestion, Roo followed. They walked a few blocks, south of the shoe-shine shop. After crossing the forth intersection, Roo was keeping count, they stopped at the fifth store-front on the block — it was a jewelers. They both paused to look in the window at the sparkling and shiny jewelry and then walked in. The small bell above the door rang. Ms. Horner, the jewelry store co-owner, walked over to them — her surname and title was typed on a black and white name badge. She quickly and respectfully acknowledged Michael: "Why, hello Mr. Author, how are you?" she asked. Ms. Horner appeared to be a woman in her early 30's. She was tall, slender, and quite professional. Roo was intrigued. He had never seen a woman jeweler before. Michael said, "Hello, Ms. Horner, how are you? I'm here to make a payment on my purchase." "Ah, yes, I'll get the paperwork. Would you like to see the merchandise," she asked. "Yes, Ma'am," Michael responded. She looked at Roo and said with a sense of confidence and pride, "It's magnificent." She disappeared briefly in a back room, and then appeared carrying a receipt book and a rich-looking ring box with a slip attached; it had "Michael Author" written on it. "Voila," Ms. Horner said as she placed the receipt book on the jewelry display counter and handed Michael the ring box. Just then, the little bell on the door rang again. Ms. Horner looked at the entering customer and said, "Pardon me; I'll be right back." Ms. Horner excused herself to attend to a prominent-looking man who had just entered the store. Roo said, "My, she seems to be a very confident and capable lady." Michael opened the box as Roo looked over his shoulder. It was a diamond engagement ring. The diamond glittered and shined as it cleanly reflected the bright lights in the store. It was beautiful; or as Ms. Horner said earlier, magnificent... "Wow; that's very pretty, Michael..." Roo said. "I'm almost finished paying for it. I plan to give it to Jo Ann on her birthday next month — fewer dates to remember," Michael said while looking back and winking at Roo. Roo said, "I thought I saw an engagement ring on her finger already. Has someone beat you to the punch?" Roo chuckled at his own joke... "No!" Michael responded — a little annoyed. "I know the ring you're talking about; her parents gave it to her two years ago. It looks like an engagement ring, but this is the real thing... I considered that it was alright for her to wear her parent's gift on her finger — it helped keep other men away until I give her the real engagement deal..." Glancing over at the jeweler still serving the other customer, Roo asked, "What did you do when you first proposed to Jo Ann?" Michael disclosed, "It was informal; I gave her a big bouquet of flowers from the 'Community Florist' store. Once I pick up the ring, I'm going to have a surprise supper at 'Big Olf's' restaurant. I want you to be there cuz..." "That will be great, Michael — I look forward to it; maybe I can invite Remy to join us." Michael gave Roo an incredulous look. Michael closed the jewelry box; placed it on the counter — on top of the receipt book — and turned to Roo and said in a snippy tone, "You just stay out of the middle of the street..." Roo wasn't moved. He gave Michael a big smile and playfully punched him on his shoulder. Michael grimaced. Michael picked up the jewelry box, opened it again and continued to admire the ring. Ms. Horner came back to the young men prepared to complete the transaction. As Roo walked to the other side of the jewelry store to look at the necklaces, Michael reported to the store co-owner: "I'll pay half of the balance now and return next month to pay it off and pick it up." "Yes, siree," Ms. Horner responded as she picked up the receipt book and began writing. "I'll write a note to myself, to have it cleaned before you pick it up: say the 10th?" "No, please have it ready by the eighth..." Michael responded. "Will do, Mr. Author." Following the payment, the young men left the store. They waved to Ms. Horner through the window. Roo elbowed his cousin's arm and ran back into the jewelry store. He had put his freshly shined shoes on the floor near the necklace display counter and had forgotten them. Ms. Horner smiled with her head slightly tilted to the side as he lifted them to his chest to show her the reason for his abrupt return. "Good-bye, Ma'am." Ms. Horner said, "Good-bye, uh," she paused, in order for him to fill in his name. "Randolph Author, Ma'am," he obliged. "Another Author, great, nice to meet you," she replied. "You have a good evening — I hope to see you again soon..." She added, "And when you think of someone special, think of 'Voila Jewelry'..." Roo nodded his head while presenting one of his heart-melting smiles. It made Ms. Horner cock her head to the side and rub the back of her neck as she watched him leave the store for the second time. Even a professional like Ms. Horner was vulnerable to Roo's charming smile. Michael was waiting for him at the corner. He called back to Roo as he jogged to catch him, with a joking tone in his voice: "I can't let you cross a busy street alone..." Roo had a smirk on his face as he proceeded to cross the street with his smart-alecky cousin.

As Michael and Roo were heading back to the house, they noticed a curious gathering on the corner, near Mr. Button's Produce Store. A man, Michael later identified as Mr. Allen, was reaching down behind a stack of apple crates. It wasn't immediately clear what or who he was reaching for; but he seemed intent upon making something move. It started quite a commotion on the corner. Mr. Allen pulled, it appeared, with all his might and then appeared to lose his grip and fell back on Mr. Button's tomatoes. The back of Mr. Allen's suit was wet with the juice of the tomatoes. Mr. Button who rushed to the entrance of his market to see what was going on, held his face in frustration once he discovered that dozens of his tomatoes had been damaged. Then Mr. Button looked down to see the source of Mr. Allen's struggle — he, too, began reaching down to help Mr. Allen. Another man raced over to offer his help. Michael and Roo, who were still an intersection away from the scene, stopped and observed. From their position, they were unable to see what the men were reaching for. For Michael, it appeared to be a live comedy act; however, for Roo, it was a bit disconcerting. It reminded him of his dream: he thought back on his dream-vision of the men reaching down toward something on the ground. He recalled the anguish and frustration on their faces, similar to what he could make out on the faces of Mr. Allen and Mr. Button. It was apparent from where he stood that the men were sweating and panting. Mr. Allen lost his grip and fell back once again;

73

this time losing his derby. "Roo," Michael said, "You stay here. I'm going over to see what's going on..." Michael placed his hand on Roo's chest as he gave the instructions. Michael rushed safely across the intersection to assist the men in what he yet didn't know was the problem. When Michael reached the other side of the street and looked down toward the sidewalk, he finally realized the source of the problem. Mrs. Allen had fallen to the ground and was having problems getting to her feet. Mrs. Allen was, as some called it, heavy-set. She out-weighed her husband by 150 pounds. It was now obvious that he couldn't bulge his wife. And now, she even gave the duo of Mr. Allen and Mr. Button a challenge. The third man that had rushed over earlier had stopped helping: he turned around and attempted to muffle his laugher. Meanwhile, as he waited on the opposite corner, Roo remembered that he still had a small apple in his pocket that he had picked up from Button's Produce Market earlier. He walked a few steps toward a couple of horses, hitched to a flat-board wagon. The horses and wagon had been left unattended; probably as a result of the commotion that had drawn Michael to Button's Market. Roo put his shined shoes on the ground and began to stroke the horse's rostrums as he watched the goings on across the street...he pulled the apple out of his pocket and allowed the horses to take turns biting and chewing on it. The two horses reminded him of Georgia... Michael ran around toward Mrs. Allen's back as the other two men continued to pull her to her feet. With great effort, Michael was able to reach around her back and under her arms. He helped finally lift her to her feet. From across the street, Roo begin to see evidence of a person's gloved hands and plump head. It's was a woman with her hat hanging off her head by a hair pin or comb of some kind. Michael, Mr. Button, and Mr. Allen were finally able to rescue Mrs. Allen from the sidewalk slab. She was physically unhurt, but probably quite embarrassed. Mr. Allen attempted to, inconspicuously, straighten his wife's skirt and then fished for her right shoe which had "squirted" off her foot and lay under one of Mr. Button's fruit display tables. Mrs. Button, the market owner's wife walked over to Mrs. Allen with a glass of water and a fan. Mr. Button squeezed Mr. Allen's shoulder and then went inside his store to retrieve a couple of chairs for the couple. The spectators soon began to disperse — but not before each checking in with Mrs. Allen. They wanted to make sure that she was okay. Mr. Anderson, a slightly built, albino man wearing an out-of-place top cap and bow tie had been playing sweet tunes on his violin for the passers-by before the incident in front of Button's Market. He paused long enough to take in the amusing sight; but then began playing "Bringing in the Sheaves" as everything seemed to calm down... Roo hadn't made an entry into his journal since arriving in Tulsa, but he considered this sight, journal-worthy. He just had to make a record of this event. A few minutes later, a man approached the Allen's in a hurried fashion. Michael joined Roo on the corner with a smile on his lips. Roo pointed to the scene behind Michael's head and said, "Look, a man just ran up to the lady you just helped to her feet..." Michael stepped on the curb and then looked back toward Mr. Button's market. He said, "Oh, that's Dr. Rothman; Dr. Jones' partner. Someone must have alerted him to the situation of seeing Mrs. Allen on the ground. I think she's okay." "Roo responded, "I hope her husband and Mr. Button are okay." They both smiled. Michael said, "Let's get to the house, they'll be looking for us." Roo said, "Okay, cuz." Then as they passed Mr. Washington's shoe-shine shop, which was now closed for the evening, Roo said, "I wonder where Remy is...she's pretty." Michael looked at Roo with an incredulous expression — but didn't say a word. They kept walking. Within 15 minutes, the Author house was in sight. Michael would be able to rest from his exhausting deed of helping Mr. Allen with his hefty wife, and Roo would grab his journal and start his entry of the amusing sight. Both agreed before entering the house that they would attempt to save Mrs. Allen some embarrassment by not informing their family of what they had witnessed. Roo thought, this was the least he could do...

They arrived at the house just before night-fall. Uncle Benjamin, Aunt Beth and the preacher were in the grand sitting room talking. Michael discovered that Jo Ann was in the kitchen talking with one of his female cousins. Once Michael and Roo entered the house and greeted everyone in the sitting room, they walked out. Uncle Benjamin looked at the preacher and respectfully said, "Reverend, if you will excuse me for a minute, I need to converse with my son." The preacher responded, "Yes, Sir, by all means..." Uncle Benjamin quickly followed Michael in the kitchen and beckoned for him. Roo stayed in the kitchen with his cousin, Jo Ann and Aunt Beth, who had stepped in the kitchen shortly after her husband. Roo noticed that his uncle and Michael hadn't stepped very far from the kitchen door — although he couldn't make out what they were saying, he could hear the sound of their heavy voices; like the hum of a distance motor. They continued to talk for five minutes before they emerged from the hall back into the kitchen. Uncle Benjamin paused just long enough to wink at his wife and then proceeded to the front room to rejoin his guest. Aunt Beth, Jo Ann, and Roo's female cousin seemed to make light of the esoteric meeting between Michael and his father, however, Roo couldn't help but wonder what they were up to. The family had probably seen a number of such mini-meetings involving Michael and his father... He finally shrugged it off and thought about his journal. He had to make his entry. It had been much too long since his last entry. He tried to remember when it was — "Um, when was it?" He remembered... He made his last entry last evening after the great program at the Greenwood Community Center. He remembered that he had saved the printed program and wrote about the various participants: the military personnel, church choir and, of course, his

Aunt Beth and Aunt Emily singing "God Bless America." It was wonderful. Although it had only been roughly twenty-four hours since his last entry, it seemed like two or three weeks — he had almost loss track. He really enjoyed recording his activities and experiences — almost as much as the activities themselves. Roo was enjoying his visit with his relatives in Tulsa. Today he caught a glimpse of the Greenwood District; tomorrow he would "broaden his scope" and take in downtown Tulsa...

CHAPTER FIVE

Saturday

May 28th

"An Exotic Adventure"

(The "other side" of Greenwood)

Saturday mornings in Tulsa seemed different as compared to Georgia, Roo thought. Maybe it was the quality of the eastern horizon. Roo noticed that he was the first one awake in the room. As he sat on the edge of the bed, he thought about his upcoming visit to downtown Tulsa with his cousins, Michael, Joe, and Kevin — Michael's nephews. As he now thought about the clothes he should wear, Michael opened his eyes and began to stretch his arms. His well-developed biceps and deltoids were clearly apparent as his deep-brown skin contrasted his bleached white, tank top, tee-shirt. He had been sleeping at the foot of the same bed with Roo. After yawning, Michael asked, "What are you doing... thinking about ole Remy again? You better not be..." he warned. Roo challenged him: "Why not, she's a beautiful girl...if I get to know her; we can have all the fruit and vegetables we can eat — and more. I'd like to squeeze her tight..." Michael, intent on ending the topic, said: "Just forget about her, there's a lot of available girls around... you'll find that out soon enough." Michael said, "Go ahead and get dressed so I can get ready...I don't won't to be late." Roo quickly dismissed Michael's comments about Remy — she was his type of girl. He picked up the clothes he planned to wear and headed out the room to the bathroom. Michael sat up in the bed, used both of his hands to massage his face, and then looked toward the bedroom door. He smiled, shook his head, and threw his legs over the side of the bed. He thought: I better get up and get my clothes ready.

Before Michael and Roo had finished their breakfast, Michael said, "Roo, here's the plan; we're going to walk and meet Kevin and Joe in front of the office on Greenwood Avenue. They should be there at 11:30. From there, we'll run across the street to Ms. Lottie's. My father wants me to drop something off with her. Maybe we can pick up soda pops while we're there for our walk downtown." Roo said, "That sounds good to me, cuz... you lead and I'll follow." Roo asked, "Michael, will we be walking near Mr. Button's Produce Market on the way to downtown?" Teasing his cousin, Michael responded, "No, cuz; that would be the long route; the shortest route to downtown Tulsa from Ms. Lottie's is blocks away from Buttons..." Michael looked out of the corner of his eyes to see if he had gotten a rise out of his cousin. He had. Roo frowned and said, "That's too bad, I had hoped..." Michael interrupted, "Yeah, I know — Remy, Remy. You had hoped that you might see Ms. Remy Gooden." Roo's face lit up, "You do know her. Yesterday, you hardly spoke to her when we passed her in the street." Michael sheepishly responded, "Yeah, I know Remy; we went to school together. She's my age. Cousin, we use to court back in high school... It's a long story." Roo pressed the issue. "Does Jo Ann know Remy?" "Michael responded, "Yeah, that's what makes the story so long... Maybe I'll tell you the story later, for now, it would be better to keep my 'yesterday' away from my 'today.' " Roo got it...but played with it a bit. "You mean that it's better to keep the 'days' apart?" Michael responded, "Check!" Then Roo continued, "And, that means that you would rather me not interact with your 'yesterday,' because I might inadvertently bring 'yesterday' crashing into 'today'?" Michael moved his right index finger in the air to form a horizontal zig-zag while exclaiming: "Check, check!" Then Roo asked, while concealing a smile, and appearing to be oblivious to the analogy that Michael had used: "Does this have anything to do with my interest with Remy and maybe bringing her to the house to visit?" Now standing in the middle of the kitchen, Michael instantly scowled and proceeded to "bear-hug" Roo's body and lift him off the kitchen floor. Aunt Beth who was sitting at the table pealing carrots casually called to Michael: "Michael, don't hurt Roo-ster..." Roo chuckled while in the air and said jokingly, "Okay, cousin, okay, I get it...put me down before I hurt you." The threat didn't jar Michael. Roo continued after Michael dropped him to his feet, "I guess I can find another source to direct my affection..." Michael smiled at Roo, now realizing that his cousin had duped him. He pretended to throw a punch at Roo's well-developed abdomen and said, "Come on..." He looked back at his mother and said, "Well, so long Mom." Aunt Beth looked up after them and responded, "Have fun and be careful; don't eat too much; I'll have supper ready for you all." They both called back, "Yes, Ma'am..." Just before stepping out the door, Roo realized Uncle Benjamin's absence. He asked his aunt: "Aunt Beth, where is Uncle Benjamin? Is he okay?" "Oh, honey, your uncle is just fine. He left out early this morning on a trip. He's due back this evening." Roo's curiosity prompted him to ask Michael for more information as they walked to meet up with Kevin and Joe. "Michael, Uncle Benjamin is on a trip?" Michael said, "Yeah, cuz, he left this morning with my oldest brother Jackson and a friend to survey a piece of land outside of town...he's been thinking about drilling for oil. We own some land and there has been a lot of oil discovered in the area. My father seems to think that there's some evidence of oil on the property. He had thought about building on the land and moving the family out, but he wants to have it evaluated for crude first — he wouldn't want to build a house on top of an oil field." Michael continued, "Roo, I have an uncle, on my mother's side, who owns an oil field; he's 'filthy' rich... Uncle Jimmy has been tying to get my father to follow up on evaluating our land for oil — it's actually not too far from his property. They think there's a real good chance there's crude below the surface." Roo's eyes got wide. He had never heard of such a thing. Roo said, "Wow, that sounds great! You could become very rich..." Michael exclaimed in a casual fashion, "Well, Roo, the family is pretty comfortable now with the success of Author Financial, but my father just considers it diversifying. He always taught my brothers, sisters and me saying: 'Never put all your fingers in one mitten — find a glove and place each finger in the 'fingers' of that glove." Michael began to expand on the saying: "That's to say, don't put all your money in a single space, like placing all your fingers in a mitten..." Roo interrupted, "Yes, I got it cuz — invest in different sources..." Michael looked a Roo with a grin on his face. "Yeah; right." He said, "Oh, that's right, you want to be an accountant like my dad; well, Roo, you're on track..." As they got close to their first destination — Author Financial — Michael changed the subject and said, "Roo, we're very young." Roo agreed, "Yeah; your right, cuz, we're young men, this is our time to learn and grow...and, have fun." Michael smiled and said, "Yeah, that's the truth; but, I mean Oklahoma, our state is young..." Roo, uttered, "Oh." Michael continued, "Our state was 'formed' in 1907. I was around six years old and can remember the excitement in town. Everyone in the house was clapping and singing... Oklahoma was made up by many Indian territories at that time. I remember my older brothers saying a few years later — during the state's forth anniversary: 'Almost seventy years ago we would have had a Negro governor.' I can still remember Samuel saying: 'Oklahoma was set aside to be a Black and Indian state.' There were over 28 Black townships... The citizens of this proposed Indian and Black state chose a Black governor, a treasurer from Kansas named Mc Dade. But the Ku Klux Klan said that if he assumed office they would kill him within 48 hours..." Michael finished, "I think you can figure out the end of that story..." Roo looked toward the ground as they walked and uttered, "Yep, the Klan have always been great intimidators... but then, so are we." Michael looked at Roo with an expression of confusion. Roo continued, "Groups and crowds intimidate, it's not necessarily the quality of the Klan, but their size, 'the group.' We Negroes, as a group, also intimidate — not by violence but by the appearance of 'force.' Numbers count. We are measured by the size of our group. A single ant is powerless and is no problem; but an army of ants can cause humans to squirm, jump and run...ask those bitten and stung by a nest of fire ants...they move as a community and collective force. Moving as a group often serves as our protection." Michael walked beside his cousin in silence.

As planned, they met up with Kevin and Joe Author, Michael's nephews. They had just arrived in front of the Author Financial Office a few minutes before their Uncle Michael. They all shook hands. Michael then led the three to Ms. Lottie's across the street as his father had directed. They all entered the restaurant. Roo, Kevin, and Joe found a booth and sat down while Michael approached the counter to get Ms. Lottie's attention. Uncle Benjamin had called ahead to alert Ms. Lottie of Michael's visit. Roo listened to Kevin and

Joe's excitement about the movie they were going to see while watching Michael's interaction at the counter. Roo noticed Michael speaking to a waitress at the counter. The waitress smiled at Michael and then disappeared into the kitchen area. A minute later, Ms. Lottie appeared. Michael seemed to chat with Ms. Lottie for a few minutes before opening his suit jacket and pulling out a pouch of some sort. Without opening it, Ms. Lottie accepted the pouch from Michael, smiled and nodded her head. Roo figured that he was merely observing a business transaction. As far as he was concerned, it was probably something they had been doing for many years. Before Michael stepped away from the counter, Ms. Lottie took the pouch to the kitchen and then returned with a slip of paper. She handed it to Michael and then smiled at him. Ms. Lottie looked over toward Roo and his cousins, and waved. Roo nodded his head and smiled. Michael placed the slip in his suit jacket pocket and walked over to his relatives. Michael said, "Okay, fellas, Ms. Lottie is fix'in the sodas and then we'll be on our way — it's already 11:45." Ms. Lottie brought the sodas to the table herself. She greeted Kevin and Joe and said, "Boys, the sodas are on the house — enjoy." They thanked her and stood to leave. Roo notice the Christmas decorations on the wall and felt a deep sense of peace. The four walked out the restaurant and were now on their way to downtown Tulsa...

Downtown Tulsa, Roo thought; we're finally here. They were dressed for town, happy and quickly closing in on their destination — the "picture show." The short western, "The Cactus Kid" starring Hoot Gibson and Charles Newton, was playing at the Rialto Theater on West Third Street. A short distance from the theater, they ran across a stunning White girl waiting near her parent's car. As they approached, they noticed her family's Negro maid lumbering back toward the car and balancing multiple bags of groceries.

Roo, in typical fashion, hurriedly stepped forward to assist the maid in carrying the groceries to the vehicle. The White girl observed and immediately admired Roo's chivalry as well as his physique as he stretched and bent — while loading the groceries. Roo soon removed his suit jacket, exposing his perspiration soaked dress shirt which was now plastered to his sweaty, fully developed torso. To the girl's delight, and his on-looking cousin Michael's chagrin, Roo's nipples where clearly visible through his wet shirt. "Careful boy," Michael called to Roo. Roo paused to take a look at Michael and his two other cousins, but then returned his focus to loading the last grocery bag. For a while, there was just muscle communication going on — no squeaking, squawking or speaking... Everytime Roo's pectoral muscle contracted under his shirt, the White girl noticed. For her it seemed that there was a delightful cat and mouse game going on beneath his shirt. She wished that she could reach out and catch both... As Roo flexed his biceps muscle — sometimes cognizant of her observation — the White girl could feel the muscles in her stomach tense and then relax. At one point, in response to Roo's dynamic muscle "display," she had to catch herself as she experienced, again, the muscles of her lower belly contract and then gradually and slowly relax. The concurrent **body interaction** was blissful...she simply had to see more; know more about this hazel-eyed Negro. She took a deep breath and slowly exhaled.

Roo quickly grabbed his jacket and flung it over his shoulder — seemingly oblivious of the fact that aspects of his chest were visible to the White girl and all other wondering eyes. Actually, very little got past Roo's attention. Roo frequently exercised and worked out with a friend in his Georgia town and enjoyed the occasional opportunity of displaying the "fruit of his labor"; that is, his toned body. He politely tipped his flat-cap to the ladies, but especially focused his attention on the White girl. As he turned to join his waiting cousins, the pretty White girl called him back to the car. "Hey there," she asked, "what's your name?" Roo removed his flat-cap and engaged her with a great sense of confidence. "Randolph — Randolph Author. My family calls me Roo," he responded. "Roo, that's a cute name." She continued, "A cute name for a cute boy..." The maid, who was busy adjusting the grocery bags in the back seat of the automobile, looked over the rims of her glasses at Roo with a stern expression and quickly excused herself. She headed off in the opposite direction to the next shop. The White girl asked, "Who gave you that name?" The three young men looked at one another, but then quickly looked at their cousin who was engaged in what they had been taught is a cardinal sin — talking to a White girl in public. The pretty girl often drew the attention of the town folks; especially the boys. Many considered her to be very attractive and appealing — head to toe. This attention was now heightened, given Roo's presence — up close and personal. The White girl seemed to hang on his every word. It wasn't long before she came to realize that the person of Randolph Author was much more than a good-looking Negro male; he was thoughtful and seemed wise beyond his years.

"I'm Victoria; Victoria Herd — call me Vickie," she said as she extended her hand toward Roo as though expecting him to kiss it. He knew better... He grabbed it with his right hand and applied a gentle amount of pressure — like holding a delicate creature in his palm. She offered Roo a brilliant smile...as bright as a bouquet of lilies. It seemed a flattering pose. Roo thought: this is different — it felt exotic; "forbidden." At this point, being a little bit closer, Roo noticed that Vickie wore a knee-high length dress which highlighted her long and perfect-looking legs. Her flesh-toned stockings made her legs appear almost bare. Vickie's silk, flower patterned hat, which opened in the back, allowed her blonde hair to flow down past her shoulders and down her back. Roo also notice her shoes...they were elegant. They were lavender lace shoes with medium heels; the straps seemed to wrap artfully around her ankle. Her clothes seemed to fit her perfectly, as though custom made for her body. Roo, in response to Vickie's question regarding the origin of his nickname, explained: "Well, Ms. Vickie," he started as he tilted his head and raised one of his thick eye brows, "I learned that my sister April, who was two years old when I was born, would look in my crib and try to play "peek-a-boo" with me. Instead of saying "peek-a-boo," it inadvertently came out "peek-a-roo." Roo stuck — I'm glad; I wouldn't like to be called 'Boo.' " Vickie was captivated... She loved his voice, his expressions; his personality. She seemed to begin seeing past his outer person... Roo's close proximity to Vickie allowed him to see qualities that reminded him of Mr. Smithson, the White banker in his town. The beautiful White girl turned the color of a rose about her cheeks. He never quite knew what prompted Mr. Smithson's color change; and he didn't immediately realize what made Vickie's cheeks become full with color... Of course, Roo knew the biology behind the phenomenon. This was a flushing of the skin. This, he realized, was the result of the movement of blood in the vessels of the face. But what set Vickie's blood to moving? Was it because she was giggling? Was it a display of her emotions? Umm, yes, Roo thought; of course, Mr. Smithson often seemed to be in a state of delight and "high-spirits" when his face hued.

The perfect unequivocal conclusion: Roo had figured out the girl's emotional state by virtue of her rosy "presentation," but what of his own emotional state? What was this feeling raging inside *his* body? He had to name it...describe it — if only to himself. It was exhilarating; moving. It was a feeling that he had never quite experienced in this way. The girl before him had to be the source. He was enraptured; almost entranced. He didn't want this moment to end. But could it last? Of course not, he thought. "Maybe we can see one another again," he said before he knew it. The girl nodded her head and whispered something in his ear, and then audibly said, "Don't forget..." This was silly, unthinkable, unimaginable; they both became giddy and began laughing... Michael, Joe, and Kevin looked at Roo and Vickie in disbelief. Their mouths were agape. Roo almost forgot that his cousins were there. For that matter, he forgot the world around him existed. Michael had seen enough; he had to intervene. He abruptly stepped forward to grab his "foolish" cousin's arm...

Before Michael could establish some sense of control over his giddy cousin, someone yelled from across the street, "Hey you 'high-falutin' niggers over there; what you doing to that girl?" The statement jarred Roo as well as his cousins. They stopped and stared across the street at the source of the demeaning comment. It was a White teenage boy with freckles who attempted to intimidate the four young men standing near Vickie. Vickie, who seemed amused at the apparent challenge, casually watched the scene play out before her. Michael instantly released Roo's arm and walked around to the front of Vickie's large family automobile. The other two boys followed their cousin, Michael, and stepped off the sidewalk — that's as far as they needed to go. Roo was undaunted as he watched from his great vantage point — near the beautiful young lady. In a single move, he placed his foot on the running board of Vickie's automobile and propped his right elbow on the side mirror. He watched as his Tulsa cousins went into action. Vickie quickly glanced at the clearly composed young man standing near her and then back toward Roo's cousins; then again at the freckle-faced boy across the street. Michael started toward the boy; looking first to the left and then the right for oncoming traffic. The boy stood, nervously staring at Michael as he approached him. He tried to look brave, courageous, and steadfast; especially for Vickie — the white girl's sake. He wasn't going to retreat, no, he wouldn't move an inch — he belonged there. It was a given, he had the support of all the town's folk; they wouldn't let him down...he could stand his ground. The boy thought, how dare those people leave their "Little Africa" and think they can take over... His thoughts were dashed as Michael's distance from him began to quickly shrink... Perspiration was beginning to form on the boy's forehead. No one walking past him seemed to be bothered with the boy or Michael — the boy's approaching challenger. Before Michael could get around the automobile — the only remaining barrier between the boy and himself, the boy shot off dropping his half-eaten apple to the ground. The boy ran as fast as he could looking back to see if Michael was in pursuit. It was at that point that the boy stepped in a heap of warm horse manure just left by a passing horse as the boy hurriedly crossed the street at the end of the block. Roo and his cousins could hear the boy cry out, "Ahhh" as he pulled his foot free of the "mess" and plodded off to safety... Michael smiled, then looked back toward his entourage across the street and shouted, "Wow, he's fast!" After a loud and abrupt laugh, Joe called back to Michael, still across the street, "The reverend always says: 'You reap what you sow.' That boy gave us 'mess' and he went and stepped in it...Ha, ha, ha, ha...hooo!" Vickie and his three cousins laughed. Michael knew that the boy wouldn't stand his ground; they rarely did when alone. Michael had no intentions upon hurting; or for that matter, touching the White boy — he just wanted to scare him. As a young adult, he knew he could be in big trouble if he assaulted a White citizen. Michael quickly realized that they had better move on — the White boy just might get the attention of a policeman and return. He turned around, quickly looked in both directions for traffic, and jogged back to Vickie's car and his observing cousins. Roo knew that although they were not in

Greenwood District proper, this was Michael's territory; he knew just how far to take things.

When Michael reached his cousins, he smiled politely at Vickie, who was sitting in her car staring at Roo — she finally acknowledged Michael with a return smile and said, matter of factly, "Yes?" Michael said before Roo could react: "It was nice to have met you, but we must get going before we miss our picture-show." He reached and grabbed his visiting cousin's arm and pulled him along. Vickie stood up with an expression of disappointment, but didn't speak. She desperately wanted to get to know Randolph Author — she couldn't take her eyes off him as the four young men disappeared from her sight. Nonetheless, she quickly remembered that she and Roo had made plans to meet again, and she aimed to be there — she just hoped that he'd follow through.

Once Roo, Michael, and their cousins rounded the corner to the theater, they stopped. Michael scolded Roo. They were in the middle of the sidewalk just in sight of the movie house. "Roo, what do you think you were doing back there? You're supposed to pay attention to my lead; you can get into big trouble here if you cross the line. It was one thing for me to chase after that White kid and another for you to talk to that White girl. They're very sensitive about their woman folk; especially, pretty ones. Don't do that again..." Michael had made his point: he could see it in Roo's eyes; however, he couldn't have known that Roo had made up his mind to see Vickie at a later time. At this point, Roo was smitten and all he could think about was the beautiful and "exotic" White female; her dimpled-cheek smile, rich blue eyes, and delicate figure.

The four made it in time to see the introduction of the movie. Once inside, they hurriedly made their way up to the mezzanine. The segregated-section policies reminded Roo of his hometown in Georgia. Nevertheless, Oklahoma was a well-to-do state boasting acres upon acres of oil-rich land. The highly valued commodity had made many Oklahomans quite wealthy — Negroes included. It afforded the surrounding communities a wealth of fine building materials, good schools, excellent eateries, wonderful shopping venues... and here, even in the mezzanine of the downtown movie theater; it provided plush seats and ornate decorations — indeed, it was a fine and well-appointed Negro section...

The theater house lights dimmed as the large screen simultaneously brightened. The sound of the large projector was audible as it ticked and clicked right above the Negro section. The images on the illuminated theater screen could be seen reflecting off the eye glasses of many of the Negro viewers... The capacity crowd in the mezzanine erupted in a roar as the title, projected in big bold letters, announced the long awaited film: "The Cactus Kid" starring Hoot Gibson. Roo, as well as his cousins, he had just learned, loved westerns; it was the way of "real men" confronted with "real-life" situations. The crowd's cheer gave way to clapping as the screen text melted into darkness. Anticipation and the thick smell of popcorn were in the air. The Author men watched the film — beginning to end — without a word to one another; they were vicariously engaged with each scene. Kevin and Joe were on the edge of their seats throughout the movie. The "Cactus Kid" held the attention of everyone in the theater — White and Negro. The film ended to the dismay of many in the audience: they wanted more of Hoot Gibson and his wonderful screen antics. The boys sat in their seats virtually exhausted. Their emotions had seemed to gallop along side Hoot's every "bend" and "turn". Kevin and Joe slowly slid back in their seats, as though sliding off the back of a horse saddle after a wild ride. They quickly composed themselves and watched two additional features – but the "Cactus Kid" reigned supreme in their minds…indeed, it was worth watching again and again. The house lights came on: Kevin was beaming; he was mesmerized… He looked off toward one of the theater's magnificent ornaments imagining himself riding with Hoot Gibson in one of the film scenes. Kevin was unknowingly chomping on a piece of black licorice he had kept hidden in his pocket (he always carried a supply inside his coat pocket). He quickly became aware of his surroundings when he noticed Joe's opened hand in his face — begging for a licorice rope. Roo noticed his cousin Kevin eating the licorice and came to realize the reason behind his always smelling like sweet medicine…

Mr. "Bumpus", the theater's piano player, had been in rare form today. His name actually was Jules Carson, but many of the frequent movie goers knew him as "Mr. Bumpus" because of his tendency to cause the piano to bump as he played it during the more exciting film scenes. At one point during the "Cactus Kid" film, the slender piano player had stood up while playing — pushing the stool over. A theater worker recovered the stool from the floor below the stage and strategically slid it right behind Mr. Bumpus' knees causing him to flop down on the stool with a thump. The piano player had continued playing without missing a beat. The White audience on the main floor of the theater roared with laugher; many of the Negroes missed the sight from the mezzanine, but had definitely heard 'Mr. Bumpus' piano playing "bump". His enthusiastic playing certainly "woke up" many of the silent films: even the most exciting scenes in movies like the "Cactus Kid" would have fallen flat if one depended on just the subtitles. Mr. Bumpus was a theater star. At times, he would stand in the lobby following his musical "performance" and autograph the patron's programs: *Your Maestro, Mr. Bumpus…*

The boys stayed seated and began discussing the exciting "Cactus Kid" scenes they had viewed — they had instantaneously become film critics. It was unanimous: Roo, Michael, Joe, and Kevin considered "The Cactus Kid" one of the best movies they had seen. Of course, as with any positive film review, it had to be shared with any and everyone interested in seeing a top-notch western. They wouldn't be disappointed — and the young men would be sure not to disclose the plot when giving their movie report.

As they stood up to leave their seats and the mezzanine area, they saw what appeared to be the top of a policeman's hat. Yes, it was a White policeman coming into the mezzanine area — the area designated for the Negro audience. Michael, Roo, and their cousins didn't pause but continued toward the opposite side of the mezzanine to go down the stairs on the far side of the theater. As they started their descent — Joe, Kevin, and Roo walking ahead of Michael — Michael looked back and caught sight of a White boy behind the police officer. Um, Michael thought, that looks like the boy he had chased earlier around the corner from the theater. He was able to duck down the stairs out of the view of the police officer. Michael was glad that there were still a number of people milling around in the mezzanine to distract the police officer's attention. His cousins, who were heading down the stairs ahead of him, didn't notice the White boy come up behind the policeman and thought nothing of it. Michael urged his cousins to move hastily through the lobby and out the doors. Without questioning Michael's directions, they all complied. Once outside, Michael led the group as they jogged around a different corner from the one they had rounded earlier en route to the theater. The group had jogged five full blocks before Michael slowed to a walking pace. Although Roo detected that something was going on, he didn't ask. He considered that it had something to do with that policeman back at the theater.

Now moving through the downtown streets at a slower pace, Roo noticed a confectioner shop. The store front had hearts, candy drops, candy-cane shapes, and a candy rainbow; in multiple colors. The window dressings, candy display, and sweet-smell was thoroughly inviting...however, Roo didn't know if he would be welcomed in the downtown store. He stood at the window looking at the candy inside. He spotted and stared at what appeared to be salt-water taffy. He stared at the taffy as he listened to the periodic ringing of a small bell over the door. The store was very busy this Saturday afternoon — a wonderful time for a family stroll and sweet treats. Michael looked over Roo's shoulder at the candy in the window display. Michael knew what Roo's question was going to be... Are Negroes allowed in this store? Before Roo could turn to Michael and ask his question, Michael stated, "No, cousin, Mr. Olsen doesn't allow Negroes in his store...bad for business, he says." "Oh," Roo said nonchalantly, half expecting the response. "Too bad," Roo responded, thinking of Brenda. "I wanted to pick up some salt-water taffy for a friend in Georgia; I guess I'll just take my money back to the Greenwood District..." Michael smiled and said, "Most of us *do, Roo*; most of us do." Kevin offered, "Roo, there's a candy shop right off of "Greenwood." I think they sell taffy — it probably tastes better." Joe interjected, "If not, at least the

customer service will be better... Let's get back to Greenwood, I'm hungry."
He finished by asking Michael, "What's Big Ma Ma making for supper?" Roo,
who was listening to most of the conversation without facing his cousins,
finally turned and looked back at Joe and Kevin. He had to remember that
although Michael often addressed the boys as his cousins, because of the
nearness of their age to his, he was actually their young uncle — the youngest
brother of their mother, Katherine: Uncle Benjamin's oldest daughter.
Michael ignored the question from his nephew — Joseph always seemed to
be hungry. The young men turned to leave — just as the confection store
owner spotted them and waved them away from the window. Roo casually
thought of his new acquaintance, Vickie, the White girl with the brilliant blue
eyes and dimples. He smiled, and thought, "I have a white friend here, who
can go into any store and pick up anything I might want...that would be
great..." Roo took his suit jacket, already hanging over his arm, and swung it
over his right shoulder. With a new sense of associated power and "privilege"
— in the person of Victoria Herd — he confidently walked with his cousins
en route to the Greenwood District, whistling a tune he composed on the
spot... Power by Association; yes, he felt even more like "Tulsa Material." Of
course, Michael could have told him that he was modifying its Author family
definition... Nevertheless, the town's White folks considered the Negro boys
and their like "Little Africa material," and were probably always glad to see
them go back where *they belonged*...good riddance...

CHAPTER SIX

Sunday

May 29th

"A feeling in the air"

Roo awoke to the smell of bacon. Ah, he could smell coffee too... He sat up in the bed, bracing himself with his right elbow. He looked toward the foot of the bed, where Michael usually slept. Michael was already up getting ready for service. It was Sunday. Roo was usually an early riser, himself, but he found that he was a bit tuckered out from Saturday's visit to downtown with his cousins. He turned his body in the bed and placed his feet on the floor. He paused and stretched his arms in front of him and then he raised them over his head. He stood up and bent over and touched his toes as though preparing to engage in calisthenics — oh, that felt good. Roo repeated the bending actions and then stood on his toes for two minutes to stretch his calf muscles. Ah, that's great...he thought. This was a good morning routine. He stepped away from the bed and began twisting back and forth. First he twisted while holding his waist; then he continued the twisting action while extending his arms. He could feel the tension on his sides and mid-section. He stopped abruptly and fell back on the bed behind him. With his back on the bed, he began to raise his legs above his body like two large parallel steel rods. He held them in this position for three minutes and then began to bend his knees toward his chest. Roo wrapped his arms around his bended legs and squeezed tight — Roo looked like a human football. He slowly extended his arms and his legs away from his torso like a jack-knife. At this point, his arms and legs extended over the sides of the double bed. He was done.

He sat up in the bed with his legs crossed like an Indian sitting in front of a teepee. He knew that he should begin preparing for service, but he stopped to think about his meeting; no, his rendezvous with Vickie this evening...He could hardly wait to see her again. He thought of his first sight of the pretty girl sitting in her family's car. He could hardly think of anything else. Of course, a few things happened while they were in town, but they seemed to pale in comparison to his memory of Vickie. The thought jumped in his mind: I'm not only dressing to go to service, but I'm dressing to see Vickie. He looked at the clock on his cousin's bedroom wall and leapt to his feet to head to the bathroom; he knew his aunt would be calling for him soon. But first, he had to pick out one of his best Sunday-go-to-meeting suits. Yes, this is the one...the dark, tapered-down suit. He would plan to place a daisy in his lapel before he headed off to see Vickie.

Twenty minutes later, Roo was sitting with his relatives at the breakfast table. Uncle Benjamin was reviewing his Bible lesson while occasionally sipping a cup of strong-smelling coffee. He was the adult class teacher. Uncle Benjamin placed his book on the table beside his plate and finished the last spoon full of grits on his plate. He looked at his wife and said, "Dear, that was delicious and filling. I hope I don't fall asleep during the sermon; heavy stomachs and monotone voices aren't a good combination for staying alert and attentive." Roo and Michael smiled. Kevin, Joe, and Jennie, Kevin's sister, spent the night and were also sitting at the table. Aunt Beth instructed, "Okay sweeties, finish up so we can get to the service; we don't want to make your grandfather late." "Yes," Uncle Benjamin agreed, "let's pray and be on our way..." Roo nodded his head toward his plate as not to let the others see his sheepish expression. Here he was in the middle of a heart-warming exchange with his relatives — before service — and he was preparing for a "not all together" honest act: he was going to sneak out of his relative's house at night-fall. Michael and Uncle Benjamin were going to an important meeting at the community center this evening — no guests or visitors permitted. His Uncle Benjamin's other nephew, by marriage, Johnson, had invited Roo to his house this evening, but Roo would decline this time around and stay in. He would excuse himself and turn in early. It was all planned... In his mind, he tried to justify it as: this is an investment in a friendship. This will be an exploration; the coming together of two different worlds — for the good of racial...cultural and social development. No one in the kitchen noticed as he placed his hand on his forehead and whispered: "Oh, brother..."

Roo was sitting toward the front of the sanctuary. He really enjoyed the service. The choir had just finished a selection and the announcement clerk stood at the podium. Sister Porter was her name. She was a tall stately-looking woman of 60. Her voice sounded as though she was speaking in falsetto. As she enunciated each syllable she seemed to wave her large, decorative handkerchief. Her hat slid to the side of her head as she looked down to read the announcements. The woman would occasionally use her handkerchief-hand to adjust the large yellow hat on her head. Roo could hear the laugher of little children in the congregation. Roo was, at first, amused; but then found that the heaviness of his stomach — the grits, bacon, omelet, and biscuits — got the best of him. The last words he heard Sister Porter utter in a high-pitched, operatic voice were, "one dollar in advance, or a dollar and a half at the door..." Roo was now deep in a dream-state... Roo was walking down a dark and shadowy street. It was gloomy and the buildings appeared to be damaged, burnt. Roo hadn't remembered this feature in his dream before. He seemed to be in the middle of an oddly familiar street. He could tell that there were figures ahead of him as well as behind him. He felt a pull to stay ahead of the figures behind him...the figures behind him felt ominous, foreboding, and dangerous. He couldn't fall behind — they might catch him; he had to keep up with the group ahead. He couldn't tell who was behind him or, for that matter, who was ahead of him. Why was he now in the dream-scape? There, again, he could see the faces of Negro men on the side. They were very sad, troubled, in pain, in anguish... This part he remembered, it was a recurring theme. The tormented faces were unfamiliar to him.

In Roo's dream-scape, the group was moving slower and slower; it seemed the faster they attempted to move, the more energy they applied, the slower the result. The group behind seemed to be gaining. It seemed that the pursuing group was prepared to pounce on them. Why were they chasing them? And, where did the pursuit began? Roo didn't know, it just seemed that they should attempt to stay ahead... They were all in the middle of the street, but there were no automobiles moving on the street, just people running, fleeing something, someone. They had to escape. His legs felt heavy, the sky was gloomy. He looked down toward his shoes — they appeared to be disappearing from sight. It was like they had melted into the pavement. Now his legs, his hips...everyone in the group that was ahead of him was also sinking into the pavement — lower and lower, deeper and deeper. The group behind was now virtually on top of them. He could now here their voices: they were yelling at them. Their words were not altogether clear, but they sounded angry. Roo could feel their fingers scratching at his back. He could hear himself demanding: "Stop it, stop it, don't touch me..." They tried to catch him and pull him back. He and his group continued to sink into the pavement until they were finally, completely underground. Their pursuers were gone, they had disappeared. The group was safe — he could hear members in the faceless group cry out, "Amen, amen; you said it brother, amen, amen...!" Roo suddenly awoke, he was still in his Uncle and Aunt's church. He opened his eyes and saw many around him standing and raising their hands as Minister Crawford preached. He turned his head in an attempt to orient himself and found that he was staring into one of the ceiling lights. Squinting, he turned his head in the opposite direction just in time to see and hear a short, middle-age deacon shout out: "Amen, amen; you said it brother, amen, amen!" Roo sat up in his seat and smiled. Wow, he thought, what was that dream all about?

Roo felt a mild sense of relief having been awaken by the sounds and voices in the church. The new features in his dream were very troubling, especially since the "dream-setting" appeared to look more and more like that of the Greenwood District. If nothing else, that is what he was definitely able to remember of the dream — the setting. Roo pulled his pocket watch from his pocket and saw that it was now 2:00 P.M. This had been his first visit to Sunday service at his uncle and aunt's church, and he didn't quite know their usual dismissal time; but guessed that it must be soon. His mind now took him to his friend Vickie...

Before he had reached the church for Sunday School and noon day service with his relatives, he had begun the count-down in his head. Hour by hour; minute by minute — he was getting closer to "rendezvous time..." The thought of disobeying his Uncle Benjamin's instruction to never leave the district without his cousin Michael had all but dissipated from his mind. The drive, excitement, and anticipation of seeing Vickie was overwhelming. Maybe, it was also the quality of doing something in secret and the risk of being caught that fueled his excitement and exhilaration. Indeed, Roo didn't take into serious consideration the enormity of the risk. He was not simply preparing to leave the all Negro district for an evening's journey into the "White" part of town; he was preparing to walk into the "lion's den" where the mother lions were always keenly aware and sensitive to the well-being of their precious cubs — Victoria Herd was the precious lion cub in the pride and every White adult in the community, the mother lion. For Roo, this was to be the exploration within the exploration; an expedition within an expedition. He left Georgia for his expedition to the Greenwood District and now he was gearing his mind to leave the district for his expedition into downtown Tulsa, Oklahoma. He was not deterred by the difficulty of the expedition: expeditions always have some amount of challenge. The only difference for Roo was that his expedition only involved one — himself.

Roo was sitting on the pew, now smiling to himself, or at least he thought he was smiling to himself. Michael, who was sitting on his right side, nudged him and whispered, "Roo, why are you smiling like that...the pastor's wife is looking at you and probably thinks that you are smiling at her." Roo looked directly toward the lady Michael had pointed out and saw that, indeed, she was looking back in his direction. She appeared to be at least 10 to 15 years her husband's junior — perhaps she was 35 years old. She was very attractive, especially in her deep, dark blue dress and matching high-heel shoes. She wore a bright, blue and white striped, pill-box hat. She was sitting in front of the church toward the side, near what appeared to be the other ministers' and deacons' wives. She certainly didn't look like the average pastor's wife. She had a wonderful white smile and looked like she should be seated in the choir stand with the other young women, as opposed to being with the other ladies who looked like they could be her great-aunts... Roo was suave and low-key. He kept looking toward the lady and gradually toned his dashing smile down to a grin. He nodded his head in order to say "hello ma'am," and then politely turned his head toward his cousin Michael. Michael, who did not push Roo for a reason for the smile, simply whispered in his ear: "Her name is Sister Earlene; she's pretty, isn't she?" Roo nodded in affirmation as Jo Ann, on Michael's opposite side, shushed him. Michael stopped talking immediately, hoping that Jo Ann hadn't overheard his opinion of the pastor's wife...

It was now time for an outreach offering. Service would be dismissed soon. The congregation on Roo, Michael, and Jo Ann's side of the church was directed to stand and move toward their right. Everyone in their row stood in obedience — everyone, that is, except Roo. Michael looked back at Roo, who was still seated, and beckoned him to follow. Roo abashedly looked up at Michael and Jo Ann, who had now noticed Roo still on his seat, and spoke loud enough for Michael to hear him over the background piano music: "I'll just wait for you here..." He handed Michael a few coins to carry to the offering table for him. Michael gave Roo a curious look and then turned to face the aisle. Michael looked a bit embarrassed when he discovered that Jo Ann and the rest of the people ahead of him in his row had already cleared the row — everyone appeared to be waiting for him to advance and head to the offering table. A stern-looking, dark-skinned lady in an usher's uniform looked first at Michael, who now moved quickly past her in order to catch up to Jo Ann who was now near the offering table at the front of the church, and then back at Roo, still sitting on the pew. She was perturbed. The rest of the congregants on the other side of Roo crossed over him with disdain — one lady almost tripped over his new shoes. Roo reached out in an attempt to catch her arm. Before she went down, she was able to catch her husband's shoulder and steady herself. This created a buzz in the audience behind them. The usher, still waiting at the end of the aisle, looked at the crowd behind and placed her left, white-gloved index finger in front of her lips while directing the people with her right hand. A little boy standing behind Roo in the next row, waiting with his parents for their turn to head toward the offering table, suddenly sneezed twice: "Ah-shoo, ah-shoo." Roo could feel the spray of spittle on the back of his neck. Roo looked back at the boy and then up at his parents. His mother looked at the boy and said in a hushed voice, "Ennis, say excuse me, and cover your mouth next time." Now, they were on the move toward the aisle at the usher's behest. Roo took out his white handkerchief and began wiping the back of his neck. He thought, maybe I should have marched around to the offering table... Jo Ann and Michael returned and carefully crossed past Roo's knees and sat down. Michael turned to Roo and said, "Now I know why you didn't want to march around the offering table; when I got to the table, there were a lot of women in the front and in the choir stand, leaning forward, half-standing, and gawking in my direction. I'm sure that they expected to catch sight of you — head to toe — even the pastor's wife seemed to be looking around the back of a deacon in my direction. Cousin, I think that there will be a lot of young females hanging around the church doors when church dismisses... the pastor will be on the inside of the doors and the girls will be on the outside. They won't let you get away without saying hello or catching a glimpse..."

Once the service was dismissed, Michael let Roo know that his parents and his mother's sister and husband were going to drive to the house, and that he would be walking with Jo Ann and him. Roo definitely didn't mind walking. He enjoyed taking in the sights. Although Michael could drive, Roo also was glad they had walked to downtown Tulsa yesterday. Had he and his cousin driven to the picture show, he would never have met Vickie. Michael was right. After waiting in line to greet the pastor, he stepped past the doors to find at least fifteen to twenty young females staring at him. They seemed to scrutinize Roo's 6'1" frame. And they didn't seem to be disappointed. What they missed at the offering table earlier, they caught at the door — the sight of Michael Author's handsome cousin from Georgia: Randolph Author. Michael noticed that even some of the older women were looking in Roo's direction. Aunt Beth would find this very annoying and distasteful if she knew about this. Michael could hear his mother's voice in his head: "Why, that's an absolute shame, an absolute shame for those women to stare at my dear nephew that way. I won't be surprised if Pastor Crawford has words about it next Sunday." After about 10 minutes, the vast majority of the females began to leave with their families — heads turned back catching their last glimpse of Roo. Two of the remaining young females, the bold ones, approached Roo as Jo Ann, Michael, and he began to walk in the direction of the house. Michael knew that many of the other girls wished they could have approached Roo. As an excuse to get a closer look and maybe an introduction to Roo, the girls called out to *their friend* Jo Ann: "Hey, Jo, how are you, sista?" Wasn't that strange, Jo Ann thought; they stood and stared toward them earlier and hadn't acknowledged her once — not even a hand wave. "Wait Jo." They ran over to where they were standing. They quickly looked over at Michael and said, "Hey." Then they proceeded to ask Jo Ann about Roo...right in front of his face. "Is this your handsome cousin?" Christian asked. "Boy is he good looking," Suzanne added. Jo Ann responded, "He's not my cousin, he's Michael's cousin, and he's standing right in front of you — just say hello." Suzanne said, "Yeah, of course, you look just like Michael." She stood in front of Roo and continued, "Hi, my name is Suzanne Swanson; my grandfather is the pastor of this church and this" — she held her hand out toward the other girl — "is Christian, my cousin." Roo responded, "It's nice to meet you ladies." He then finished, "Ladies, we have quite a long walk ahead of us, but it would be nice to see you both again soon, what do you say?" The girls batted their eyes, looked at one another, and said in unison: "Yes, we would love that..." Christian added, "Are you staying at your cousin Michael's house, or with other relatives?" "I'm staying with Michael," Roo answered. "I'll be here for a few weeks; I'm spending the summer with them." "Great," Suzanne said. "Maybe you and Michael and, oh yeah, Jo Ann, can come over to my grandparent's house for dinner — I'm a good cook..." Jo Ann tilted her head to the side and thought: well, well. Jo Ann grabbed both young men's arms and without looking in their direction, told the young ladies, "Okay, Suzanne, Christian; nice talking to you, we have to go — so long..." They were off to meet with Michael's parents and other relatives at the Author house. Michael knew that he wouldn't be at home very long once they arrived; he and his dad had an important meeting to attend. They would drop Jo Ann off at her house after a short dinner and then head to the community center. Unfortunately, this time, they would have to leave Roo at the house with his aunt and other relatives. Michael thought: we'll make it up to him... Of course, unbeknown to Michael, Roo already had plans...plans that would take him to a different domain. However, he didn't realize how different that domain would be.

After dinner at the Benjamin Author household, the family and relatives began to disperse. As Uncle Benjamin and Michael made their way out the door, Michael could hear his Uncle Carter's son, Daniel, who was the same age as his oldest brother, ask Roo if he wanted to join them at the local picture show. He heard Roo decline and report, "I think that I'm going to turn in early tonight..." Michael thought to himself, well, good; then Jo Ann and I can take him to the picture show later this week and maybe take him to a Greenwood restaurant. Uncle Benjamin opened the door on the passenger side of the automobile and climbed in; placing his cane on the seat between himself and Michael, who was in the process of starting the engine. Jo Ann hurried out of the house and climbed into the car and sat behind Uncle Benjamin. Roo stood on the porch with his Aunt Beth and cousins Kevin and Joe, who stayed behind — they had expected to spend some time with their cousin, Roo. Kevin and Joe had come to enjoy their Georgia cousin; especially after their visit to the downtown picture show. They had considered Roo's interaction with the White girl daring. He seemed like a guy that would never avoid a good challenge... They stood and watched everyone leave the house. It was a quiet and comfortable evening. Aunt Beth, Kevin, and Joe went into the house while Roo stayed on the porch a few minutes longer. He could feel the anticipation growing in his being. He was going to see Vickie, as planned; in 45 minutes. He caught the last glimpse of Uncle Benjamin's automobile as it rounded the corner. He thought, boy; my relatives have it all together...then he heard the car backfire in the distance. He smiled and entered the house.

It was 6:15 P.M. It was almost time to leave. He had it all planned. He would excuse himself from his relatives in the front room and head to Michael's room. From there, he would climb through the large bedroom window. He would be able to spend, at least, an hour with Vickie. It wasn't a lot of time, but he knew it would be blissful... "Okay, time to engage the plan," Roo uttered in a whisper.

The time had come: after a deep breath, Roo said, "Aunt Beth, I'm going to the room now. Can I be excused?" Aunt Beth hugged Roo and said, "Alright, honey." Roo said with a smile, "I'll see y'all in the morning..." Aunt Beth smiled but didn't speak. Kevin and Joe looked at one another, back at Roo, and then continued playing checkers and drinking pop. Roo continued, "Aunt Beth, no need to check on me, I'll be okay..." "Okay, dear," she responded. It was Kevin's move on the checker board, but he now quickly and with great youthful agility turned on his back — propping himself on his elbows — and looked at Roo with an expression of curiosity. Joe tapped Kevin on the shoulder and said, "Come on, move your man..." He paused then returned to his game with Joe. Roo walked into the bedroom and gently closed the door behind him. Roo thought: Maybe I over-did it, at the thought of suggesting that Aunt Beth not check on him...especially when Kevin turned to look at him. Um, anyway, at this point he thought of how much time it would take him to reach the rendezvous point, the amount of time he would spend with Vickie, and the time he would need to be back in order to beat Uncle Benjamin and Michael to the house — 8:50. He wouldn't have much time to spare. He stared at the window he was preparing to exit...he was about to second guess his plan and decision to leave the house. Suddenly, he heard the phone ring. It rang again — and once again. I better wait, he thought. A minute later, Aunt Beth called for him: "Roo; Roo, telephone..." "Ah," Roo said under his breath. He took off his jacket, that he had put on in preparation for his journey and removed his shoes. He opened the door and hurried across the room to his aunt, who was holding the phone toward him. "It's April," Aunt Beth announced. Before finally handing the phone to him, she bent over to the transmitter and said, "April, sweetie, it was nice to hear your voice; Auntie loves you..." She smiled and nodded her head as she listened to April's response. She handed the phone to Roo. Aunt Beth quickly returned to the kitchen to pull cookies out of the oven. He heard Kevin call to his grandmother: "Big Ma Ma, can I have four, while they're hot?" Aunt Beth shushed Kevin, and said, "Kevin don't talk so loud; Roo is on the phone. Come and get your cookies..." Roo smiled and then spoke in the transmitter while placing the conical shaped receiver to his ear. "Hey, April, how are you?" April said, "Roo, everything's great here; mom and dad are doing good...they're still very busy — as usual. We all miss you and can hardly wait for you to come home. Are you having a good time in Tulsa?" "Yes," Roo responded. "I miss you all." Roo couldn't bring himself to say that he might want to live in Tulsa. He said instead, "Tulsa seems to be a real nice place." April asked, "What were you doing before I called?" Roo twisted his lips and looked up at the ceiling — a dimple formed in his right cheek. "I was going to step out," he said. He thought; there should be no harm in telling her that. "Oh, where are you going, bro?" April asked. Roo should have known; April was often very inquisitive. "On an expedition around the town," he responded. That should satisfy her, he thought. It did. "Okay, I won't hold you, have fun," she paused and finished, "be safe brother, you're my only one...we love you." "I love you too, sis." They hung up. He placed his hand over his nose and mouth and thought: what was that about...why did she call me now? He finally turned and said, "Aunt Beth, thank you, I'm going to the room, I love you." "You're welcome honey..." she replied. She began to hum a church tune he had recalled hearing earlier at the church service. He now began to feel a little guilty at the thought of sneaking out... Aunt Beth's voice was amazing.

Roo looked over at his cousins eating cookies and playing checkers. He returned to the room and put his shoes on. He grabbed his suit jacket and climbed out the window. Roo hunkered down outside the bedroom window and paused. The smell of black licorice had penetrated his olfactory sense. Umm, he thought, I must have walked past Kevin's coat in the front room – the coat in which he kept his licorice stashed. The licorice smell immediately reminded him of one of his less enjoyed experiences in downtown Tulsa; the limitation and restriction placed on him and his cousins at the confectionery shop. He remembered the face of the merchant through the window change from "kind" and "pleasant", as he served his White customers, to "disgust" and "exasperation" as the merchant noticed the four dark faces peeking in. Roo also remembered the way the merchant abruptly shooed them as he turned away to leave with his cousins… "Oh well", he muttered. He quickly attempted to clear the thought and the lingering hint of licorice in his nose. He was on his way to meet with Victoria Herd...no turning back now.

Indeed, Roo was on his way... He determined that he would be able to easily find the location that Vickie had specified yesterday. Roo would have to get back to the point where they had first met — where she had her family car parked. Once there, Vickie told him that he should walk to the end of the block and round the corner to the left. There, he would see a beauty parlor called "Puddintangs." The parlor, she indicated, was right across the street from the alley entrance. "Puddintangs" was the landmark... These directions, Roo mused, were all mentioned in the form of a whispering in his ear that afternoon. He fondly remembered the way her warm breath ticked his ear as she whispered the words...

After a few minutes of walking at a brisk pace, Roo was on the edge. That is, without knowing the exact boundary of the Greenwood District, *he was crossing over*... This must be the boundary, the line: Roo noticed a few make-shift signs that he hadn't noticed yesterday when he and his cousins returned to the district from the picture show... One said: "Little Africa, U.S.A." Another one, painted in red letters on a black background, said: "Nigger-town." Another said: "High Falutin Dump." The last sign he saw before he lost interest said: "Hazardous area – Enter at your own risk..." Before he arrived to cross over the railroad tracks, he thought: What is the meaning of those mean-spirited signs? Was it just a color or race thing, or was it more? Roo had seen many signs and symbols in Georgia pointing to the White folk's disdain for Negroes but here, one of the signs was a little different. Now having crossed the tracks and heading due west, he recalled the "High Falutin Dump" sign. Was that a reference to the overall wealth within the Greenwood District? Were the White folks looking at the economic standing of the Blacks in the community? Was this an added point of contention for them? Roo quickly reflected on his uncle's discourse following his first family dinner with his Tulsa relatives: You are the "social" *thermometers*; you reflect the social conditions for them. His forehead and eyebrows furrowed as he pondered his uncle's thoughtful sayings — however, at this point, he failed to consider his uncle's first and major point during that same setting — *"Don't Cross The Line."* Roo had already crossed the line from the Black side to the White side, i.e. the Greenwood District to

Downtown Tulsa, but now he was en route to crossing a major *"fault line"* — he was heading straight on into a meeting, interfacing, rendezvous with a White girl: the universal "treasure" of White society...

CHAPTER SEVEN

Sunday

May 29th PM

"The forbidden rendezvous"

Where was she? Have I been set up? Maybe she didn't really have feelings for me — were the thoughts that rolled around in Roo's head. I know she told me to duck into the narrow ally between the Brady and Starlight Buildings on the west side of the street. Roo was glad the store-fronts were dark. The streets were deserted. No prying eyes, Roo thought. He felt bad for sneaking out of Uncle Ben and Aunt Beth's house, but he had to see the beautiful White girl once again. I can't believe that I've betrayed my relatives... Maybe I should head back before I'm missed. At that moment, Victoria Herd entered. "Were you about to leave, Roo Author?" she asked. "Yes, when I didn't see you, I thought maybe I was in the wrong place: I still have that feeling." Roo stood still with his arms folded across his chest as Vickie moved toward him and extended her right hand and arm in a fashion that allowed her to hook his waist and dance around him clockwise like a little girl swinging happily around a flag pole. She was thrilled as she felt the form of his masculine belly, ridged sides, and the curvature of his lower back. The circular motion began pulling his neatly tucked dress-shirt out of place. His bare belly was exposed as his shirt twisted in the direction of her circular passes. She spread her fingers like a fan in an effort to touch every inch of his torso. Gradually his shirt moved upward. She could feel the solid knobs of his spine. Roo's biology, as his dad often referred to it, became animated. The third time around, Vickie's ring finger caught his navel — she issued a deep gasped. Roo gently grabbed her hand... She stopped and giggled. Now behind him, Vickie slyly, but quickly, inserted her fingers into his loose fitting pants and yanked hard at the waistband of his trousers in an attempt to force them open. Roo kept his balance but lost a button as it popped off into the darkness...the second button remained intact. Vickie smiled, and then laughed. For the moment, Roo felt almost inanimate, like a human-sized "play-thing." Nevertheless, Roo soon changed his mind about leaving — he was beginning to feel more comfortable in Vickie's presence. Vickie moved away and led him to an area further away from the alley's entrance. Roo thought: this is risky...yet, he followed like Mary's nursery rhyme lamb. As he followed her deeper into solitude, he began tucking his shirt in. He didn't notice Vickie take delight in sniffing her cupped hands. She had touched his soft, Negro skin. She had never touched dark skin before, not even her maid's. Ummm, she thought, her hand smelled good — he smelled good. Roo used mineral oil on his skin thinking that this was what Jack Johnson, his all-time favorite boxer, used before his boxing matches.

That feeling had come once again, he loved it. Roo felt his sense of reason leaving him. Vickie, he noticed, began their secret visit as a "lily" but again became a "rose" as her cheeks exposed the influence of his presence. This can't be wrong. *Is* it wrong? Why is it wrong to befriend this girl? "You know we could get into big trouble for being seen together," Vickie warned. "Yes," Roo responded, "it seems that one would have to travel much farther than a train could journey to leave the prejudices behind." "Maybe the moon..." Vickie offered. Just then, Roo brashly and impulsively disclosed: "Vickie, when I met you yesterday, I had a feeling inside that I've never experienced before. I felt like I didn't want you to leave." Vickie responded, while gently biting down on the corner of her bottom lip, "Me, too." At first sight, Roo thought Vickie was extraordinarily pretty. She was tall and thin with flowing blonde hair, and perfect teeth. Vickie was also seventeen; born two months before Roo. Dimples formed in her cheeks every time she smiled, which was often. She had a habit of often biting the corner of her lip in a coy fashion. The faint freckles around the bridge of her nose seemed to solidify her adolescent innocence. Her eyes were extraordinarily blue and seemed to have a depth that could overtake the largest of earth's creatures. Roo tried to take it all in. He tilted his head back and looked toward the darkening sky above. He thought out loud for the benefit of his new adoring friend. "I remember back home in Georgia, I was at the local barbershop waiting for a hair cut. I listened as two gentlemen debated over the wonders of the 20th century. One of the men said, 'This is the 20th century, a new age; a new era.' He said, "This is the century where men will begin to see eye to eye, Negroes and Whites. We've moved from the century of slavery and bondage into the century of freedom, understanding, and new attitudes'. The other man said, 'The men you speak of have not started out in this century; they have crossed over the 19th century line into the 20th century, and they've dragged with them their old ideas, ways and practices.' He said, 'The understanding and new attitudes you speak of doesn't come simply from the passage of time, but from the forming of relationships.' " Roo continued by echoing the barber's sentiments: "New attitudes come from the forming of relationships." Roo raised his arms and interlinked his fingers behind his head. He noticed Vickie admiring his chest and biceps. Um, he thought, maybe I do look like my dad. Just then they heard a shifting of the boxes and crates behind them. Vickie looked back with an expression of fright. Her lily-white skin returned. Roo, although nervous didn't show it. He looked back and forth in an attempt to track the shuffling sound. With the pose of a hunter he stooped in a crouching position and proceeded toward the point of the noise. Where did this innate quality of courage and bravery come from: Mazumba? Just then, a stack of crates and boxes crashed down around him as Vickie looked on in horror. Three dark figures leapt out to pounce on Roo, who was prepared to engage in battle. Vickie stifled a scream as she recognized her brother Rascal, and his two friends Billy and Jack — all three fifteen. They were recovering from being knocked down by Roo who had quickly tripped all three with an abrupt leg swept. Roo knew that his time spent with Mike Wiggins — a former Army soldier who taught him a few "moves" — would payoff. Vickie called to Rascal, "What are you doing here?" Rascal, brushing himself off, shouted back, "What are you doing here with this nigger?" Billy and Jack were on their feet and ready to jump Roo. Vickie shouted, "Stop, stop! Leave Roo alone!" Roo was again prepared for battle. When the boys spotted Roo's "battle pose" and unrelenting stare, they backed off. At once, Vickie remembered that this location was not only her secret hide-away, but also Terrance's, aka: Rascal. Much like Roo's story a day earlier, Vickie was responsible for her younger brother's descriptive nickname. When she was seven, she overheard her father referencing a critter that seemed to follow his hunting party during a hunting expedition. Her father had always referred to the animal as "the little rascal." He would say, "The little rascal would follow us and then disappear until we opened our food supplies; and then, once our backs were turned, the little rascal would help himself to our beef-jerky, fruit, and other snacks. We couldn't get rid of him; and the little rascal seemed too domestic-like to shoot...he was quite mischievous." Yes, that was the name for Terrance: "Rascal." Boy was he mischievous. It was actually Rascal's mischievous exploits that forced Vickie to share this, her "sanctuary of solitude" with him in the first place — but yet, maybe it was a mischievous deed on both their parts...

At the age of 13, Vickie had climbed down a large trellis off her second floor balcony to meet with Scott Wallace, a "cute" classmate of hers. Vickie was unaware that like her dad's pesky follower during his hunting trip, Rascal, whose room shared the same balcony, noticed Vickie's risky climb down the flimsy wooden structure and proceeded to follow her. However, when he got a third the way down the trellis, in stealth fashion, the trellis broke loose from the balcony and crashed down onto a large, well-trimmed bush which cushioned his fall — but didn't muffle his scream. Rascal had survived the fifteen foot drop. Wrenching from the pain of the fall, he looked across the lawn near a small grove of trees in time to spot Vickie with a look of shock with her hands still on Scott's bare chest, and Scott with his hand under her blouse. Scott had an expression of horror as he looked toward Rascal with a face smothered with Vickie's lipstick. If only she had disappeared quickly and taken Scott to her sanctuary as planned; she had thought at the time. Now, the hiding place was Vickie's valuable negotiating piece. She recalled making a spontaneous deal with Rascal before their parents arrived to investigate the situation. She promised to share the location of the hideaway — "a great place to play pirates, hey" — if he took the rap alone. The young boy agreed, but paid dearly by suffering the "rod of correction." Scott had shot off to his house while Vickie ran to the opposite side of the house and quickly entered through the kitchen screen door — the Negro maid, "Mildred," had ignored her entry. While Rascal didn't suffer any long-lasting injuries from the fall, he was scratched up and too shaky to take flight with his sister. True to her word, Vickie later took Rascal to reveal their, now shared, place of secrecy...

Tonight, four years later, she again found herself at the "bargaining table" with her brother in an attempt to curtail the potentially profound complications of her parents learning of her boy-focused intermingling. "Let's make a deal, you don't tell on me and I won't tell on you," she bartered. Rascal and his friends had been chewing Jack's dad's tobacco and drinking a stolen bottle of Billy's dad's Scotch. As socially "evil" as her interactions with a Negro male was considered, she determined that Rascal's antics, especially given this period of alcohol prohibition, was just as forbidden — and disgraceful; particularly for a doctor's son. "You know, Terrence," Vickie said with a sassy quality, "this is very serious; you're a young boy drinking liquor." She continued with special emphasis, "And during prohibition: I'm your sister and should tell Father and Mother anyway for your own good — we can't have an illegal drunk in the family..." Vickie was striking hard; she used her brother's given name, Terrance, and the prohibition angle to her advantage. Roo observed the one-sided verbal negotiation in awe. Actually, Rascal didn't have a chance. Vickie used her wit and tongue in a fashion akin to a surgeon's scalpel. Within a period of two minutes, the operation Vickie performed on her brother seemed to have effectively and successfully "excised" Rascal's will and desire to report her presence with Roo to their parents.

As Vickie badgered and threatened Rascal with regards to his mischievous deeds with Billy and Jack, Roo noticed that Rascal's eyes got wide and began to bulge. Quickly, without missing a beat, Vickie turned to Jack, John Aires, Jr.; and proceeded to smile and wink at him. Jack, as well as many boys who saw Vickie, admired her for her beauty and spunk. Although her physical cues were remarkably apparent, her verbal comments were concealed in the form of a message whispered in his ear. He blushed and smiled at the whispered proposition. She finished with Jack by saying, "You remember what I said, Jackie..." Then, again, switching her attention, she addressed Billy, William Bennett. "Billy, your family could, and probably will, get into a mess of trouble around this: your dad is a judge — this wouldn't be good for his image. How did you come by that bottle of alcohol; is it your father's?" Billy shrunk as Vickie got uncomfortably close to him. He could feel her warm breath as she spoke the cutting words. "Well, is the booze his?" She stopped once she determined that she wouldn't have a problem with him... It worked. It was apparent that the earlier, high-profile presence of Roo had all but disappeared. He was no longer the focus of attention for Rascal, Jack, and Billy — Roo had become invisible in their minds. Each could only think of Vickie's persuasive and invasive words. After Rascal and his friends walked away, with no more than a flippant and exasperated hand wave, Vickie turned to Roo and said with a victorious smile, "Nurse, hand me the sutures, we can close them up..." Vickie had never been in an operating room, but she had heard many surgical words from her dad. Roo didn't know if it was due to his fisticuffs with Terrence, Billy, and Jack, or the awesomeness of Vickie's performance, but he needed to sit down for a minute. He wasted no time finding a crate that had been knocked down during the scuffle.

Roo stood up after a brief recovery period and said, "Vickie, I'm glad we were able to see one another again, but I should be heading back to the Greenwood District; my relatives will notice my absence and come looking for me." Roo, who was left incredibly vulnerable by his feelings for Vickie, was more so, taken aback at Vickie's response: "No, you stay here with me or else!" Vickie's statement was made brashly and boldly — it was cutting. Roo thought, what happened? Vickie was the offspring of a well-to-do surgeon; indeed, affluence was not restricted to the citizens of the Greenwood District. She was born with, what most in her circle would say, a "silver spoon in her mouth." Her father had practiced for nearly 20 years as the head surgeon in an out-of-state hospital before relocating to Tulsa. Shortly following Vickie's birth, Dr. Herd practiced at the Tulsa Hospital on W. 5th Street and Lawton. He later transferred to The Physician and Surgeon Hospital on Carson and 13th Streets. In 1916 he split his time between the Physician and Surgeon Hospital and the (then) recently opened Oklahoma Hospital on W. 9th and Jackson Streets. Before long, in 1918 to be exact, he added the Morningside Hospital to his surgical rounds. He was well-known and highly respected in Tulsa and beyond. Dr. Herd was always well-received by all he met, Negroes as well as Whites. Literally, every door in Tulsa was "open" to this prominent surgeon. This was good given his frequent house calls to follow up on his patients. Vickie was accustomed to observing her dad's professional and social interactions. Dr. William Herd was known to sometimes clamp his teeth down on his thin French pipe and peer over the rims of his glasses before giving stern instructions to attending nurses, who he sometimes felt weren't moving fast enough. This often happened in his office prior to his preparing for a surgery case. The nurses usually responded accordingly; "Yes, Doctor," before darting out in compliance. In the shops and stores around town, Dr. Herd would usually enter and clear his throat as if to announce his arrival. He was accustom to receiving the best service, and often demanded such. "I would like to speak with your manager," would be his instruction to the store clerk. This request didn't necessarily indicate a problem with the front-line staff; he just felt he deserved to receive his service from the "top employees" in the company. He taught his children, Vickie and Rascal, saying: "One in authority should always interface and receive service from others in authority. In this way you never have an occasion to look down upon people; you look across at them..." Dr. Herd exuded authority and social power. It wasn't often that his was ever questioned or challenged.

Yes indeed, Dr. Herd was Vickie's authoritative role-model. Who holds the power? This was the thought that jumped into Roo's mind. Vickie's command reverberated in his head. Roo was at a loss for the first time in a long time. He hadn't had much experience with a situation like this at home. People rarely talked about power. He once remembered Mr. Smithson mention the phrases: "power dynamics" and "power differential." At first, Roo didn't know what this meant. But he felt that it was definitely coming into play here with Vickie. "My boy," Roo remembered Mr. Smithson say, "you must always be acutely aware of the dynamics of power. There is such a thing as power differential and one must stay on top of it." Mr. Smithson continued, "As the bank president, I hold power over the bank workers and the bank operations. I must carry myself as a person of authority; however, when I am visited by the bank's county superintendent, he holds the power. Indeed, I am his underling in these moments. Imagine, my boy, the situation when I am called to meet with the superintendent along with my workers — our shared underlings; together. Who would you say holds the power? Here, you must handle yourself in the midst of the power differential..." Roo's thoughts quickly centered on his current situation with Vickie. He felt powerless. Vickie Herd, the girl with the appearance of adolescent innocence, held the power. He was in her territory. She was a White girl, he was a Negro boy. She had witnesses to their company: Rascal, Billy, and Jack. She held the advantage. Roo was in a situation that he could not immediately find one way out, let alone two as his father had taught him. He was very much aware of the horrors that Negro men faced when accused of "disrespecting" a White woman. Although women were not all together as highly regarded in society as compared to White men — they had only just received the right to vote with the passage of the Nineteenth Amendment one year earlier — they were supreme when compared to Negroes; male and female. Vickie watched Roo in silence waiting for a response. Roo finally broke the silence, "Vickie, I'm enamored with you. The brief time I have been in your presence I have found it hard to part from you. Do you feel the same for me?" Vickie smiled, then bit softly on her bottom lip and gently responded, "Yes, Roo; that is why I said that I want you to stay here with me." "Well then," Roo confidently stated, "we must avoid all barriers to our being together." Roo was now extraordinarily articulate. "We can't invite anyone to learn of our meeting: your father, your mother, your friends, or authorities — they would protest and separate us in ways we wouldn't want to think of. Now, I must leave as quietly as I came; with little notice and attention. This will leave the door open for our future visits." Vickie was a smart girl, and realized that he was right. She liked Roo. Actually, she found that she was also enamored with him. Any use of the social power and advantage she knew she held over him would take him away from her — forever. "Let's plan our next visit," Roo suggested as he looked over his shoulder. When he turned back to get a response from Vickie, she presented a rosy-cheek, dimpled smile and leaned forward to whisper meeting plans. Before leaning back from his ear, she kissed him on the cheek...she again took advantage of her proximity by grasping his sleeve-concealed biceps. She squeezed both of his biceps firmly, now standing in front of him. Vickie was a tall girl but her head only reached

Roo's neck — his Adam's apple, to be exact. She quickly advanced and passed the palms of her hands across his chest; the chest she had earlier admired from a distance. She could feel the firm, symmetrical mounds of Roo's pectoral muscles under his shirt. She instantly raised his shirt to further investigate his muscular form. Just then, she stopped and aggressively passed her hands and arms past his arms, which he positioned like two large loops as he rested his hands on his waist. She hugged him tightly. She rested her head on the sternum of his chest — she could hear his rapid heart beat; she could feel her own heart beating — it seemed to beat in unison with his. Her long blonde hair, which was pulled back and meticulously styled begin to cascade down around her shoulders and face. In like fashion, the shoulder strap of her dress slid down her right, shoulder exposing a faint "sprinkling" of freckles and her bra strap — she didn't care. Vickie was enraptured. Roo noticed, Vickie smelled "rich" or at lease what he imagined White-wealth might smell like. She smelled like flowers — a bouquet of freshly picked flowers. She was becoming "unkempt" before his eyes — she seemed ultra-relaxed. He was **moved**... Vickie was also moved: she was moved in a way that was not immediately measurable by Roo — her "mover." The blood flow began to quickly infuse and saturate the sensitive tissue of her bosom — beneath her garments — she could feel the rush...the sensation in her breasts... The right cup of her bra was now clearly visible to Roo as her dress continued to shift downward — he could see the flowered pattern of her undergarment. Her bra appeared to fit loosely along the top of her breast. Roo could now see the smooth white skin of her right breast rise and fall under the loose cup as she took in deep breaths. Vickie was on the verge of swooning. She wouldn't have minded Roo touching the skin of her partially exposed breast... But Roo knew better. This was remarkable, shocking; Vickie's actions seemed uninhibited and unrestrained. It was as though she had forgotten that she was in close, intimate contact with a Negro; the "butt" of society. How could her actions be so fluid toward him? Vickie bit down on the corner of her lip; then smiled and looked away from Roo's face, toward his buttoned pants. She could feel the gradual movement of his body-part between their bodies... Before she knew it, she whispered a quick, "Oooh" and began to muse...

...Mischief was definitely a Herd family trait... Vickie was now aroused beyond reason. Roo was exotic ... gorgeous ... perfect; unblemished. Her unbridled thoughts cried out in her head: I want to see more... I have to have more...more; more...her face was flushed and contrasted her blonde hair. She began to shift her weight toward him. She began to usher Roo backwards; he yielded. His feet shifted along the floor — not knowing their destination. Then, suddenly, Roo lost his balance; he was down on his back with a thud. Roo was stunned — he saw stars before his eyes. Roo had tripped over a piece of wood that was on the floor following his scrap with Vickie's brother Rascal and his friends. He hit the back of his head and was semi-conscious. Vickie, who earlier had a tight grip on him, was lying on top of the dazed young man. She was unhurt in the fall: his muscular body had cushioned her. While Vickie had no intentions on Roo being injured, this was her way of getting him to the floor...she wanted to lay on the floor with him. She propped herself over him with extended arms, while asking if he was okay. Roo, attempting to open his eyes, rolled his head back and forth on the wooden floor. He grimaced in pain, but appeared to be quickly recovering from the bump on the head. Vickie straddling Roo, which drew her dress up to her thighs...was now gingerly sitting on his closed legs. She didn't care what "flesh-toned" colored unmentionables Roo spotted as her dress slid up her long, stretched legs. Vickie turned her attention back to her "ploy of passion": like a little girl with the mind of striping her play doll of it's clothes in order to see the hidden territory beneath; began attempting to unfasten and lower Roo's pants. Roo cleared his head and was able to muster up enough strength to interfere with Vickie's effort to lower his pants — however, not before she was able to open the button and expose the front of his white boxer underwear... Vickie paused and looked upon Roo with delight. She visually inspected the form and shape of his

underwear against his body as they hugged his thighs and lower abdomen, just below his
smooth-looking belly button: they fit perfectly. Now, like the intrigue of a man looking
under the hood of his running automobile, Vickie watched the movement of Roo's abdomen
in concert with the band of his underwear as he inhaled and exhaled...she visually took in
all the inter-workings before her. Roo appeared to be embarrassed. Now, using his weight
advantage, he was able to raise himself with his strong arms and slightly bent knees —
lifting Vickie up as she slid down his legs to her feet. He quickly fastened his pants and
tucked his shirt in — sliding his hand in and out of his pants in the process: she watched
the motion of his hand in his pants with a sense of pleasure... Before he knew it, like the
opposite pole of a magnet, Vickie was attached to him. She grabbed him around the waist a
second time... (Alas, Vickie's 43 second "daydream" faded — they hadn't fallen to the
floor; Roo wasn't dazed; and she hadn't actually peeled his pants open to see his white,
perfectly-fitting underpants...it was her imagination. She was still standing pressed against
Roo and his "body-part": Indeed that was real.)

The mood shifted too soon for Vickie. Roo's identifiable passion for Vickie
changed. It was now tempered by her earlier distasteful display of
manipulation. Roo uttered, "I should go now," he paused, "…in order to
return…" He gently placed his hands on her waist and delicately guided her
body to the side. His hands informed him that she was quite fit. Vickie looked
up into Roo's eyes with disappointment on her face. Vickie wanted to
continue her exploration of the handsome young Negro standing before her.
Indeed, Vickie had, during their brief interlude, used her eyes, ears, hands,
and even the closeness of her body to his in an attempt to glean, gather, and
take in the person of Randolph Author. Beyond his being a Negro, she
wanted to know what made him tick. She was immeasurably intrigued. Was it
animal magnetism? Was it carnal "insatiation"? Of course, but even more, it
felt deeper; it was spiritual. In Vickie's eyes, Roo seemed taller; gigantic. Roo

demonstrated remarkable restraint as he examined Vickie's person in a more vicarious and subtle fashion — essentially using only his eyes and olfactory senses to experience her. He had long understood the difference in social entitlement and privilege when it came to Blacks and Whites — especially with those of the White, female "persuasion." In contrast, Vickie's actions were forthright and unabashed. Roo returned an expression which Vickie interpreted as: remember, for the sake of our future visits, others must not know of our meeting; the meeting of our hearts... Roo's expressions were often salient and descriptive — and seemed to transcend even racial and cultural boundaries. After a few minutes of mutual staring, Roo displayed his dazzling smile. With a voice that projected a strong quality of authority and control, Roo announced, "I have to go." Vickie longed to kiss Roo's lips; what must that be like, she thought. He departed before she had the chance. With her head tilted to the side and wonderment in her eyes, Vickie began adjusting her dress and pinning her hair in place. As she turned back to watch Roo depart she spoke out softly, "Next time Randolph Author, next time..."

Roo was confident that he had dodged a bullet. He was certain that he had Vickie's confidence and secrecy with regards to their meeting — he had touched her heart; the core of her being... Indeed, Roo was right; although he hadn't touched or examined the body of the 17-year-old — with the "salient" blue eyes — as his mind desired, he *had* touched her in a profound and lasting way. Unbeknown to him, as Vickie took the first steps in an attempt to leave their place of rendezvous, she paused, crossed her arms over her stomach, closed her eyes and quivered. Randolph Jefferson Author had transported Vickie to the point of ecstasy and back. However, Roo couldn't be so sure if Vickie had secured her brother Rascal's confidence. Rascal's heart wasn't quite as accessible... ultimatums don't usually reach as deeply as heartfelt experiences. While he had found pleasure in being in Vickie's presence, he knew he had to leave, and leave on his own terms — he had somehow effectively handled himself in the midst of the power differential. Now, he had the "power" of Uncle Benjamin to face back in the Greenwood District.

CHAPTER EIGHT

Monday

May 30th

"Dream Fragments"

He hit him like a ton of bricks. "Wow, what could be causing this feeling?" He was again recalling aspects of his dream... it was even more palpable...it was visceral. There was a feeling of dread building in him like he had never experienced. He couldn't shake it. To this point, Roo had considered his dream-vision as a troubling, but neatly packaged message from his subconscious — everyone had those. But now, it seemed more like a premonition...a forewarning of things to come. Like an arthritic old man whose joints are sensitive to the change in atmospheric pressure and inspecting the heavens for developing precipitation, Roo stopped and began to slowly and methodically look around. It was as though he was looking for someone. Michael came into the room in time to catch Roo's bizarre action. "Roo, what are you doing; what are you looking for?" Without pausing, Michael asked, "Are you okay?" Roo ignored Michael's inquiry, and then as though just realizing that Michael was in the room, stopped just short of bumping into him. Roo asked, "Oh, how long have you been standing there?" Michael grabbed Roo by his broad shoulders and demanded, "What's the matter with you, bro? You have a strange look on your face and you're sweating... Are you ill...I'll go and get my mom...she can attend to you." Roo didn't respond. Before he knew it, Aunt Beth, Uncle Benjamin, and Aunt Emily were in the room inspecting him. Aunt Beth held her hand to his head and then abruptly left the room to bring him some hot tea. Uncle Benjamin guided Roo to the bed and aided him in sitting down. "Son, what's wrong...is it the heat?" Roo, sitting with his shoulders slumped and his head down, finally moved his head toward his uncle and said, "Uncle Benjamin, I don't know what's happening to me...I just feel as though I have been slugged in the stomach by Jack Johnson. I don't feel sick, but it is physical." Aunt Emily, who had followed her sister out the room, came in with a damp, tepid face cloth. She instantly sat down on the bed next to Roo and placed it on his forehead. She began praying silently. Aunt Beth came in with a cup of hot tea. "Drink this Roo..." Then asked, "Where is that castor oil, Ben?" Uncle Benjamin looked back at Michael and Kevin who had just entered the room and said, "Michael, get the car and bring Dr. Jones to the house; right away..." "Yes, sir," Michael responded. Both he and Kevin rushed out of the room and the house toward the family automobile. It was a blazing hot day in the Greenwood District. Roo's relatives encouraged him to lie back on the bed.

Twenty minutes later, Dr. Jones walked into the bedroom behind Michael — Kevin followed. Dr. Jones looked down at Roo and noticed that he was soaking wet from perspiration. Uncle Benjamin assisted the doctor in removing Roo's shirt. "Randolph," the doctor called. Roo slowly looked in the doctor's direction. He seemed lethargic. Dr. Jones checked Roo's pulse, heart beat, and the condition of his eyes; then instructed Aunt Beth to chip some ice from the ice box and bring it to the room. As Aunt Beth and Aunt Emily rushed out the room to comply with the doctors instructions, Dr. Jones called out, "Oh, and put some cold water in a 'hot' water bottle and add some ice in it." They returned to the room within five minutes. Dr. Jones had given Roo a pill and began placing the chipped ice over his head and on his neck. He took the "hot" water bottle filled with very cold, ice water and placed it on his bare stomach. Roo didn't even flinch when the cold elements touched his body. "Mrs. Author," the doctor spoke in a normal voice, "please prepare the bath tub with ice and cold water — just in case..." Aunt Beth stepped out once again to comply with Dr. Jones' instructions. Soon they noticed that the color was coming back in his face and chest. Roo began to respond. "What happened to me? I remember saying something to Uncle Benjamin and that's it. Dr. Jones, what are you doing here?" Roo asked. "Randolph, you just lay here quietly and you'll be just fine — for some reason you were going into shock..." Dr. Jones winked at Roo and said, "I don't know what caused it, but we stopped it — in its tracks; you should be just fine." He walked out the room with Uncle Benjamin, leaving Aunt Beth and Aunt Emily to attend to him. Indeed, Roo felt much better. Michael and Kevin were in the background observing their cousin. Before leaving the house, Dr. Jones recommended that they keep the ice pack on Roo's stomach for one hour. Uncle Benjamin nodded his head in affirmation. Then in response to Uncle Benjamin's offer to get him back to his office in the family automobile, Dr. Jones said, "Ah, thank you, my friend, but I think I'll walk — I need to stop in and check on Mrs. Farmer around the corner. I'll plan to see you tomorrow at the committee set-up meeting, right?" "Right," Benjamin

Author responded. Uncle Benjamin watched his doctor friend exit the yard. No one was around at the moment to witness his perplexed expression as he turned from the door.

Later that evening, Roo was lying on the bed with a light blanket covering him. Uncle Benjamin was sitting in a chair on one side and his oldest cousin Jack, Michael's oldest brother, was sitting on the opposite side of the bed. Jack said, "Roo, you gave the family a scare...when I heard, I had to rush over and check on you. Boy, we're not use to seeing a healthy, strong guy like you get sick like that..." Uncle Benjamin touched his shoulder and asked, "Roo, do you remember what happened just before you fell ill?" Roo thought, now that's a good question. He responded to his uncle, "I had these troubling thoughts and then I felt weak." "Do you remember the thoughts you had before you felt weak?" Uncle Benjamin asked. "Yes," Roo responded. "They were thoughts of danger and trouble...it felt to me to be a warning...a warning of some great tribulation." He paused and then continued, "Here; here in Greenwood..." Roo finished, "At one point, it seemed only to be troubling dreams, now it seems more like a premonition." There was now a troubled looking expression on Uncle Benjamin's face that both Roo and Jack noticed. "Dad," Jack said, "now, what's wrong with you?" Uncle Benjamin fell back in his chair; Roo sat up in the bed as Jack stood and headed to his father's side. Jack called out, "Ma Ma! Come here and bring a glass of water — come right away..." Within minutes, Aunt Beth and Aunt Emily appeared at the door with a glass of ice water. Aunt Beth was surprised to now see her husband being attended to. She approached Uncle Benjamin and abruptly asked, "What happened?" She handed the glass of water to her husband who sat up and elevated his hand as though taking an oath; to indicate that he was alright. Aunt Beth with Aunt Emily standing at her side placed the glass to her husband's lips and forced him to take a drink. After taking a few sips, Uncle Benjamin assured the family that he was fine and briefly reported what had come over him. "It was something Roo said that shook me. His experience was awe-striking: it seemed to have effected me physically." Roo, who had turned his body in the bed and placed his feet on the floor, was instructed by Uncle Benjamin and Aunt Beth to lie back down. Uncle Benjamin stood up in a display of steady strength and walked past his family to the door. He looked back at Roo in the bed and said, "Son, I'll be back to check on you..." Aunt Beth, Emily, and Jack looked at Roo, and then followed him out.

A lot had just happened. Roo wondered why his uncle had had such an adverse reaction to his story — he was left to ponder the question. Soon, Roo's thoughts switched to his own somatic experience. He considered that maybe the severity of his symptoms was due to his disobedience to his uncle and aunt. He had ventured out on his own to visit with Vickie after night-fall; that, after being instructed by his uncle not to leave the Greenwood District without Michael. Although his uncle never approached him, Roo had had a feeling that Uncle Benjamin knew of his absence from the house. Roo now came to realize that maybe ***"it's the not knowing what is known about you by others that can eat at you."*** Did Uncle Benjamin know? Roo was "stewing"; this was a quandary that added to his immediate discomfort.

Indeed, Roo had come to realize that something very wrong and troubling was approaching: Tomorrow? The next day? He couldn't answer that question; nonetheless, he felt eerily confident that something would happen. There seemed to be a point of no return; a time-junction that had been crossed that changed his dream to a premonition. Even that was unclear.

However, it was becoming evident that his Uncle Benjamin had some significant role to play in the *imminent event*. His mind wouldn't allow him to leave the multiple questions of...what, how and when? Maybe it has to do with the weather — a storm; yes, severe storms in Oklahoma were common in the spring to summer months. Oklahoma was known for its tornados; twisters. Tornados could be devastating. Maybe that's what was behind the visions of the troubled Negro faces. Of course, what else could it be? Living in Georgia, Roo had seen a few tornados in his lifetime. As brutal as the tornados were, the folks had always known what to do and where to retreat — whether at school, in town or at home, they always survived. If a storm or tornado was the source of his troubling and tormenting feelings, he knew that they would be able to survive. But, survival did not account for the tearful Negro men in his dream-vision. Then; what?

Later, Roo heard the front door open and close; it was Michael returning from the office. His fiancée Jo Ann was with him. Michael had taken a break to check on Roo's condition. As Michael approached the room, Uncle Benjamin intercepted him. Roo could hear part of the conversation. Uncle Benjamin asked Michael, "Son, did you see to the chairs and cots that were delivered?" Michael responded, "Yes, sir. I asked the men to place them near my desk; I'll take them from there..." Uncle Benjamin stated, "Very good, Michael. I know that it's hard work, but it will be well worth it...for the good of the family and the good of our friends." The conversation ended and Michael finally entered the room. "Hey, cuz." Michael expressed with an appearance of relief. He was glad to see Roo upright and animated. "It looks like you're doing a lot better; I was worried about you." Roo responded, "I'm okay Michael; I'm ready to get back to downtown Tulsa. I want to take in some more of the sights." Michael retorted with an air of sarcasm, "Son, I think you've taken in more of *the sights* than is safe in these parts for a Negro…" Roo, was ready to offer a response, but then abruptly stopped himself — like slamming on the brakes of an automobile to avoid running over a wayward animal crossing the street. Roo was jarred back in thought: what was Michael referring to…his interaction with Vickie, the pretty White girl, downtown near her car on Saturday afternoon, or their secret meeting behind the downtown buildings — last evening? By this time Michael, oblivious to the fact that Roo was deep in thought, had his back turned to Roo and was looking out the bedroom window: he was still talking… Still engaged in deep thought, Roo's conscience seemed to respond to him in a snippy, "smart-aleck" fashion — *of course* Michael is talking about the Saturday afternoon meeting. How could he know about the secret meeting… Saturday's meeting; that's the only thing he knows about you and Vickie: *come on, son…* His conscience had let him have it. His inner-person finally released him just in time to hear Michael's last words while still looking out the window: "…We're going to a restaurant tonight; I want you to come and meet Jo Ann's sister, Janice. She's pretty, tall, and smart; just like you — that is, "pretty"…like you; get it." Michael smiled, not realizing that Roo didn't get the joke. Roo suddenly realized that he zoned in just in time to receive an invitation to dinner with his cousin Michael, Michael's fiancée Jo Ann, and Jo Ann's sister. What could he say? Michael turned away from the window and walked toward Roo, who had gotten out of bed and was now standing in the middle of the room. Without waiting for Roo's response, Michael faced Roo, clutched his broad shoulders, looked him in his hazel-colored eyes and said, "Shake it off and be ready by six." Michael walked past Roo, toward the bedroom door and called back, "Oh, Janice told Jo Ann that she caught sight of you Saturday when we stopped by the candy store to pick up the taffy … she said that you were gorgeous, something or other…" With that, Michael exited the room with Roo still standing in the middle of the floor. Roo realized how much Michael was like his father, Uncle Benjamin. Michael could be light-hearted and engage in a little levity, as when he crossed the street to scare the young White boy while in downtown Tulsa on Saturday and, yet, he could be quite serious and imposing. Roo thought, it's good to be an "Author man"... Then Roo spoke out loud: "And, I better be ready for dinner by six..."

Roo had finally met Jo Ann's sister — he was sitting face-to-face, across the table from her. She was definitely her sister's sister. She bore a strong resemblance to Jo Ann — physical facial features and personality: Roo thought that in Aunt Beth's words, she was "sweet." She had a wonderful disposition. Yes, the sisters seemed to have all things in common; sitting side-by-side across the table from him and Michael — similar smiles, long hair, bright eyes; that is, until they stood up to walk to the garden patio. Roo estimated that Jo Ann's sister towered over her by at least two inches. She could easily look at Roo eye-to-eye. At this moment Roo was grateful for his height — so was Janice. "District" guys were intimidated by her height, stating: a man just shouldn't have to tip on his toes for a kiss...

The restaurant, "Starbrights," was one of Greenwood's finest. It was located around the corner from Michael's house. It had fancy tables, beautiful window dressings, and an ornate piano in the middle of the restaurant floor. The dimmed lights gave the establishment a warm and comfortable ambiance. The maître d' was a handsomely dressed, tall Negro gentleman with wavy hair. He always addressed Michael and Roo as "young gentlemen," and Jo Ann and Janice as "gracious ladies." He was very attentive. They engaged in idle chatter for the first few minutes as they listened to the guitar music in the background and then all decided to move to a different venue. They all left their table to sit in the garden while they waited for their meal. The music was great. By this time a woman dressed in an evening gown joined the guitarist on the piano. Janice asked Roo, "Are you enjoying yourself; I definitely am..." Roo seemed a bit puzzled. He responded, almost as just having arrived in the middle of an event, "Oh, yes, Janice, this is a nice restaurant. Did you and your sister select it?" Janice said, "Yes, my family and I come here often to celebrate our special events: anniversaries, birthdays, and graduations. We usually invite Michael to come along... He's like family already," she finished. Jo Ann smiled in the background. Michael interjected, "Jo Ann and I are thinking about having our wedding rehearsal dinner here." He looked at Jo Ann and said, "We should get an early start and make reservations." Jo Ann was ecstatic. She simply leaned forward and hugged her fiancé. Both Roo and Janice looked at the couple with large smiles. Roo was trying to enjoy himself. He was in good company; but, Vickie had him... Roo couldn't get her off his mind. Roo felt as though he was two-timing her. They had had such a wonderful and deep experience with one another. He felt that it was beyond physical, it was spiritual. He had never experienced such a feeling before. Of course, he had been with other young females in his time, but no one had ever brought him to his proverbial "knees." Roo understood that the fact that she was White and he was a Negro had something to do with the attraction and quality of their relationship. It was "exotic," unusual, atypical... different. In his mind's eye he could visualize that way Vickie's half-exposed right breast moved as she breathed. "Uh; what?" Roo suddenly called out... Michael nudged his cousin who seemed to be daydreaming. Jo Ann and Janice didn't notice Roo's distant stare: they were giggling and chattering about the wedding rehearsal dinner. "It will be here before you know it," Roo heard Janice say as he "zoned in." Michael said in a hushed voice: "Roo, are you a dreamer or are you a thinker?" He tried to imitate the preacher who had questioned Roo a few days earlier. Roo's immediate response was interrupted by the maître d's announcement, "Young men, gracious ladies, your dinner is served; please come to your table..." It was a great segue for Roo's response to Michael — "I'm about to be an eater; watch your fingers." They both laughed, stood, and in tandem held out their hands to aid the ladies to their feet. Jo Ann smiled at Michael and took his hand, and Janice smiled and grabbed Roo's arm. She sighed as she felt his muscular biceps and triceps under his jacket sleeve. She thought, "I could get use to this..." The couples followed the tall gentleman into the restaurant and over to their table. They noticed that their glasses had been refilled with sweet tea and their steaks were awaiting them. "Ah, that smells great," Roo said. He continued, "You know, I think that I could get use to being in Tulsa; I've really enjoyed my visit." Janice was thrilled at Roo's announcement: she looked at her sister with a smile and winked. They all sat down; this time Michael sat side-by-side with his fiancée Jo Ann, and Roo sat side–by-side with Janice. Michael looked over at his cousin and thought: I knew they would hit it off — Roo knows a good person when he sees her...

After finishing their scrumptious meal, Michael looked at his watch and said, "Well children, it's getting late, and I have to join my dad at the office early tomorrow morning — something important." The young ladies sighed in dismay but understood. Michael left ahead of the group to get Jo Ann's automobile; he was driving. Janice whispered in Roo's ear, "I really enjoyed myself — I hope we can get together again..." Roo smiled and then looked over to see Jo Ann also smiling. Michael rounded the corner and stopped abruptly in front of the restaurant. Michael had already paid the tab. Roo opened the front door for Jo Ann and the back door for her sister Janice. He stood back and watch as they climbed into the vehicle. "What a gentleman you are," Janice said to Roo. "I know...," Roo said jokingly. Janice took his response as a joke and giggled. The foursome were off to Jo Ann and Janice Crosby's house on the edge of town. The young ladies' father asked Michael to drive their car to the restaurant — he said that it hadn't been out of their garage in a while and needed to get an "outing." Michael would drop his fiancée and her sister at their house, and keep their car over-night at his house. He would return the car later tomorrow: he had planned to wash it for Mr. Crosby. He really liked their father, and their father admired Michael.

They arrived in front of the Crosby's house. It was a large farm house on the edge of town. Jo Ann didn't live in the Greenwood District. Michael and Roo got out of the automobile and escorted the women to the front door. Mr. Crosby opened the door as they climbed the front steps. "Hey there," Mr. Crosby said. "Y'all got back just in time for some home-made pudding." Jo Ann asked, "Did mom make her special pudding?" "Yes siree," Mr. Crosby responded. "Come on in everyone and get a big help'n..." Michael held the door open for the ladies — they paused before going in. Roo waved to Mr. Crosby and said, "Good to see you again, sir." He had only met Mr. Crosby three hours earlier when they came for his daughters. Mr. Crosby smiled and beckoned for the young men to enter. Michael stood outside the door and said, "Mr. Crosby, thank you for the invitation, but Randolph and I need to get back to the house. My dad and I need to get to the office very early tomorrow." Mr. Crosby asked, "Are you boys sure you won't join us?" "Yes, sir," Michael said. "Maybe Mrs. Crosby can save some for us..." Mr. Crosby laughed and said, "I'll ask her to do that." Before turning to head to the automobile, Michael assured Mr. Crosby, "Sir, I'll take good care of your car — don't worry about a thing." Mr. Crosby smiled and said, "Son, I'm not worried; I know that it's in good hands — thank you for cranking it up and taking it out for me..." "Oh," Mr. Crosby said before the young men walked down the steps, "you boys be very careful; I hear that something's going on in town. Don't know exactly what — but be careful just the same, you hear?" "Yes, sir," they both responded. Michael and Roo got in the car and pulled off as the young women waved from the porch. Roo looked back in time to see Janice blow him a kiss. Roo thought, oh brother... As the boys rode quietly back into Tulsa and the Greenwood District, Roo didn't think once of Janice; or of Remy for that matter. His thoughts were of Vickie: Victoria Herd. What was it about Vickie that made her stick out in his mind the way she did? It had to be much more than her pretty face, dimples, blonde hair, and fair skin... Vickie had character; she had style; she had his heart.

Michael pulled the Ford into the yard and said to his cousin, "Well, here we are sound and safe..." After greeting Aunt Beth and Uncle Benjamin, who were still awake and talking in the front sitting room, Roo and Michael soon turned in. It didn't seem to take Michael very long to get to sleep. For Roo, it seemed that as soon as the lights were off, he could hear his cousin's heavy breathing. Roo couldn't easily go to sleep. He reflected on his experience earlier in the day, the dream; the premonition. Dare he say that he was almost afraid to go to sleep? What would tomorrow bring? Well, he considered that only his thoughts of Vickie could help him overcome the thoughts of impeding doom. He employed all of his mental energies toward visualizing his friend Vickie — her blue eyes, her smile, her figure, her waist, her long and delicate fingers, her confident voice, and probing hands: he was sleep...

Uncle Benjamin couldn't sleep. Aunt Beth, his wife of 40 years, said, "Ben, come to bed, you must be very tired..." He responded, "Indeed, honey, as always, you're right; I am very tired, but I can't sleep. I feel a bit edgy, uncomfortable; troubled." Aunt Beth pressed him for details. "Ben, troubled about what — is there something going on at the office?" "My dearest," he started, "yes and no. I'm sorry that I caused you concern. Everything will be fine: I assure you." Aunt Beth had an incredulous look on her face, but trusted her husband. "Okay, then, let's get to bed..." Benjamin Author turned out the lights in the sitting room and followed his wife to their bedroom. This day for the Authors had been filed in their family "history book" — it was behind them. However, Benjamin Author, the patriarch and wise leader of the Tulsa family, lay on his side, in his bed: his back toward his wife, thinking about the reported activities in town... "This may just be the beginning of our sorrows." Yet, deep down, he looked forward to the next day. He remembered that the "Good Book" said: "Don't worry about the things of the morrow for the morrow will (take care) of itself..." He had a deep-level belief that all would be well. He said a silent prayer, rolled over on his back, looked at *his* Bethany, placed his hand on top of his sleeping wife's hand, and fell off to sleep.

CHAPTER NINE

Tuesday

May 31ˢᵗ

"The upside-down smile"

Indeed, something was wrong...something was happening in Tulsa — a different type of day was afoot. The Citizens of the Greenwood community seemed less jubilant; a bit somber: even the children seemed to display melancholy expressions. Just as planned, Uncle Ben and Michael had gotten an early start. They had both left for the office before sunrise. Uncle Ben had left instructions for his wife, Roo, and a few family members who were at the house to stay put: "Don't leave for anything," he had admonished. They didn't quite know what was going on, but they knew to comply with Benjamin Author's instructions.

This day seemed longer. It seemed to stretch for "ages"... Aunt Beth looked at the grand clock in the front room as she passed back and forth between the kitchen and bedrooms. On occasion, she would stop and gaze at the clock. At one point, Roo could hear her say: "Oh, my, that clock is one tick from time standing still." Roo, thought, Aunt Beth is right...save for the sound of the ticking clock, it almost seemed that time was standing still. There were no conversations, no telephone calls — what on earth was going on? Uncle Benjamin and Michael had been gone for hours — there was no word...

All day, and there still was no word — not even within the house. Aunt Beth was atypically quiet. The silence was broken when Mr. Hadden, the next door neighbor, knocked. Aunt Beth looked out the window and opened the door. Mr. Hadden said, "Hello, Ms. Bethany, how are you... how y'all doing over here?" Aunt Beth responded, "Mr. Hadden, we're doing okay." "Good," he replied. "Where is Ben, what is he going to do?" Aunt Beth responded, "Ben is in town, he should be back sometime soon: what do you mean by 'what is he going to do'? Do about what, Mr. Hadden?" The proverbial cat was now at the opening of the proverbial bag and Mr. Hadden was about to let it out... "Well," he started, "I heard that one of our Negro boys was messing around with a White girl, downtown. The word got out that the girl accused him of hurting her...the White folks are looking to hang him. And I hear that White mobs are coming into the district." He politely touched Aunt Beth on the shoulders and said, "Well, Ms. Beth, I better go. Erma and the kids are waiting for me. We're heading out of town to her sister's until this blows over — be safe..." He replaced his hat on his head and left Aunt Beth standing in the middle of the grand front room in disbelief. She quickly shook herself and thought of her husband, Ben. She knew that he was aware of the problem and would be home as he promised. Two hours later, the sun was setting. Now, Aunt Beth looked concerned...she began to pray in earnest. Roo quietly observed it all. He tried to process it all. He respectfully and reverently rose to his feet and headed to the bedroom. It had been an extremely long and eerily quiet day: the sort of quality given to the stillness before a great storm.

Reflecting upon the news of the eruption of "social chaos," Roo immediately thought out loud, "Am I responsible for this upheaval, despair and destruction? Did I create this problem for my uncle, kin, and their community?" He was consumed in his thoughts...all he could think of was his brief, but profound meetings with Vickie Herd — the White girl. It was exotic. He remembered his comments to Vickie on Sunday evening and spoke out loud, "It seems that one would have to travel much farther than a train could journey to leave the prejudices behind." He continued to think out loud on Vickie's response to his discourse that evening, "to the moon" with a sarcastic tone. Indeed, even at the age of seventeen, Roo was becoming a deep thinker: It would be an attempt to escape the inescapable...I would be leery of the other passengers on that "moon-bound" vehicle. He looked out the bedroom window, toward the darkening sky, and thought; attitudes and prejudices always move along in the minds of those who hold such beliefs — like mind-embedded suitcases. The escape can't be "geographic." It can't be an attempt to move further and further away; as in a way of, somehow, going outside and closing the door. It has to be a move in the opposite direction — a move toward entering a person's mind, thoughts, and beliefs. It would have to be an inward, internal, inside journey and adjustment from the attitudes of prejudice. Then, it hit him, like a wayward flying insect colliding with his head while fleeing a deadly swatting; again, reflecting on his conversation with Vickie that evening — that "vehicle" would have to be "a relationship." Roo realized that this had been the "vehicle" he had journeyed on with Mr. Smithson, the White bank president at home in Georgia and, yes, also Vickie: his new "exotic" friend. Just then, his deep and profound thought pattern was pierced as his cousin Michael abruptly entered the room with a serious expression on his face. "Roo, there's a storm brewing..." With a voice of deep concern, Michael continued, "The White people are stirring." Roo apprehensively responded, "I've heard..."

Unbeknown to Roo and the great majority of citizens in the district, several Negro leaders where in downtown Tulsa and began to organize for the possible necessity of defending an accused Negro assailant from a lynch mob. The police prepared to repel the possible mob. The chief of police had the accused assailant transferred to a detention cell in the county jail, on the top floor of the courthouse. The county jail was considered by both the city's police and sheriff's departments to be easily defendable. Soon, Negro men began to gather to "face the lawless White men." A crowd of three hundred White curiosity-seekers formed around the courthouse. The courthouse crowd soon grew to over 700 men, women, and children.

The sheriff reported to the top floor and began to station deputies throughout the building to protect the assailant. Later the sheriff and another man reported to the first floor of the courthouse in order to repel three men who entered the building.

Michael's report to Roo was sketchy. While he knew of the crowds of White people gathering at the courthouse, he wasn't quite sure of the target of their "malcontent." He learned that a Negro man was in imminent danger of being lynched; but didn't know if the man was at large or being detained; if he was in the Greenwood District or downtown. Uncle Benjamin was at the Greenwood District Community Center with a few of the Negro military personnel in an attempt to get the latest news. Uncle Benjamin had sent one of his sons with the band of Negro leaders to assist in the negotiations. He knew that he would receive reliable, accurate, and timely information from Samuel.

Samuel Author observed a "company of armed and hostile" Negroes as they marched up the street to the jail. They had come to offer their services to the authorities who had the accused in custody. They wanted to protect him from a lynch mob, such as the one that had hung Roy Belton, a White man, a year earlier. The sheriff and one of his Negro deputies convinced the Negro men that they were not required, and that they should return home quietly. The Negroes left. By 9:00 PM, it was reported that a fight broke out involving 150 White men and 300 Negroes.

Things were becoming more tenuous. It seemed that conditions were deteriorating. The sheriff effectively barricaded the prisoner, himself, and his men into the office. The White crowd continued to grow as several carloads of armed Blacks arrived at the courthouse. Approximately 75 men got out of the cars. Their arrival sparked a great deal of shouting, harsh words, and insults between the crowds of Whites and Negroes.

Major James Bell was alerted by a Sergeant Payne and Private Canton of B Company that armed men were converging on the courthouse. After talking to the Sheriff, he ordered the men at the armory to remain (there). The Major gave the order that the remainder of the units be notified as best as possible to report to the armory. The Major (then) returned to his house to get his uniform. He was later alerted by a runner that a mob was trying to break into the armory. The mob was driven back by Captain Van Voorhis, and Sergeant Leo Irish of the police department. Another report came in indicating the mass organizing of armed Negroes near a local plant. It seemed that the chaos was becoming ubiquitous throughout the city... Back at the Greenwood District Community Center, Uncle Benjamin listened intently for information from a retired Negro Army sergeant; he knew that he would be able to provide the most accurate news. He also knew that his son Samuel would have a sensitive hear for the "timing."

Captain Van Voorhis was at the armory when the call finally came in from the sheriff's and police department asking for help to stop the rioting. A patrol officer fell into a large crowd of armed Negroes who threatened to lynch him. His life was saved by a preacher — they let him go. The Greenwood District's street was full of Negroes; a number of them were armed. They were standing in groups talking. A few Author family men were among them. *It started*... Soon, the city-wide posturing erupted into melees. A White man was killed by a stray shot through the head, and a Negro man was injured as a police detective began firing his gun. Samuel, still at the courthouse, learned of reports of fights breaking out — two wounded Negroes were taken to the police station. Suddenly, there was a loud noise in front of the courthouse:

First, one shot, then three triggered the battle.
Four White "lynchers" died, and many more

144

were wounded… a White deputy was attempting
to disarm one of the (Negroes) when the gun for
which they were wrestling discharged…a lawyer
came inside and announced that there were a lot
of armed Negroes outside. The sheriff and a
number of deputies went out to find a large
White crowd with women and children, and a
large (Negro) group. The (Negroes) were being
headed back toward Boston when a gun was
fired… the mob broke into two groups, one
moved east to Main, then North. On the west
side, there (was) general fighting. (There were)
about a hundred Whites pushing the (Negroes
northwards)…

The time had come — the battle had begun. Uncle Benjamin began calling
family and friends. He began instructing those on the other end of the
telephone line what to bring and where to meet. As always, his family didn't
fail to respond once he gave the word. Uncle Benjamin had the respect and
complete loyalty of his family. Of course, some already knew of the rising
tension downtown, but didn't exactly know what their patriarch had in mind.
Samuel was able to safely return to the district with little to no trouble. Uncle
Benjamin gave him his seat and allowed him to catch his breath. Finally,
Samuel uttered: "Dad, it's bad, I've never seen anything like this…there seems
to be fighting and shooting everywhere — both Negroes and Whites are
being killed. It looks like things are going downhill fast at the
courthouse…they're losing control. They will probably be calling in the
guardsmen…" Uncle Benjamin paused and then responded, "Son, go home
and pick up your wife and family and meet us at my house. I'll plan to leave in
a few minutes to pick up your mom, Michael and Roo…I'll call the rest of the
relatives before I leave." Uncle Ben finished, "Son, be safe…"

The train from Oklahoma City to Muskogee was
stopped at the Katy Station…and was held.
Negroes were retreating from the south past the
station. (A pursuing) armed White mob
contained large number of teenagers, women,
and men, many under the influence of whiskey,
who were out of control and wildly shooting.
The mob boarded the train and removed all
Negroes from the segregated cars. (Negroes)
trying to surrender and those in the streets were
randomly killed.

The clock in the Community Center's director's office began to toll — it was

midnight. Ms. Sally Blue, the director's assistant, looked at Uncle Benjamin in

time to see a tear course down his cheek. She continued to watch him as he

used the back of his hand to brush the tear away…she, oblivious to the fact

that she was still in the middle of a phone call, stared at Benjamin Author and

placed the receiver on the phone hook. She had never witnessed Mr. Author

cry. This was a defining moment. Ms. Blue had heard that Mr. Author was an

early settler in the district. He, Aunt Beth, and their four older children had

moved to Tulsa from Georgia in 1894. He had been the first in his family to

move to Oklahoma. He never regretted it. For now, he finished his mission in

contacting his family and friends and then urged everyone in the community

center to evacuate for their safety. His district…his world, was being turned

upside-down. The great 1906 quake of San Francisco, 15 years earlier, had

seemed to reach the foundation of his beloved Greenwood District and

violently shake the hearts of men… Uncle Benjamin hugged a couple of

people; then squeezed the shoulders of a few others as he headed to the door.

He stopped and looked back toward a bulletin board in the front office — it

was bordered by Christmas decorations. He thought on the conversation he

had with Roo after they had picked him up from the train station. He whispered: "A symbol of love, respect... and joy — indeed." He walked through the door with the "Welcome" sign painted on the glass. He climbed into the family automobile and quickly headed to the house.

"Thousands" of Whites — armed men and inquisitive women — amassed to quell an uprising of (Negroes). At the same time, "Thousands" of (Negroes) (were) amassing north of the Frisco station. In the district, a White pedestrian was beaten when he attempted to pass through... Shortly after midnight, the Whites attempted to burn down the buildings protecting (Negro) snipers. Later, 500 Whites exchanged shots with a force of (Negros) who were firing from a "two-story shack." Four Negroes were killed; one White was slightly wounded. "Shacks" (on the) north side of the (railroad) tracks were set on fire.

Aunt Beth knocked at the bedroom door. Michael said, "Come in." Aunt Beth said, "Boys, there's a major problem." She looked at Michael and said, "Your dad called and asked us to be ready to leave when he gets here... Samuel said that it's very bad; things are out of control in downtown and that there are dangerous crowds heading to the district. You boys put your jackets and hats on... and come to the kitchen to help me quickly pack a few things." Before she could finish giving Michael and Roo instructions, Jo Ann entered the house and headed toward the room. Michael saw her and asked, "Jo Ann, honey, are you alright?" She replied, "Yes, a little shaken at the news but I'll be alright." With tears in her eyes, Jo Ann hugged Michael as Aunt Beth used both hands to massage the back of her neck. "Sweetie," Aunt Beth started, "where is your family; are they okay?" "Yes, Ma'am; my parents, Janice and younger sister Charlotte left town three hours ago. They're going to stay in

Oklahoma City with my uncle and his family until things blow over here. My parents wanted me to go with them, but I insisted that I wanted to be with Michael... I assured them that I would be alright and ran out before they could stop me. If we get through this, I'm sure I'll hear from them about my action." Michael said, "Honey, I'm sure they're worried about you, but you know that I won't let anything happen to you...you just stay by my side." Jo Ann asked, "So what are we going to do, barricade ourselves in the house?" Aunt Beth said, "No, honey; Michael's dad is on the way to pick us up — we're going to head to safety. The other family members are also on their way..." She finished before she turned to head to her bedroom and then the kitchen, "Ben didn't give me any details, but I know that he'll know just what to do — he always has." Michael wiped the tears from Jo Ann's cheeks and then kissed her on the forehead. Michael looked back at Roo, who observed the exchange and waved for him to follow him to the kitchen. They all walked quickly through the grand front room of the house and into the kitchen. Aunt Beth had already placed three crates on the table before alerting Michael and Roo about the situation. Aunt Beth called to them as she walked toward them from the front room: "Pull as much as you can from the pantry." Just then, Uncle Benjamin opened the front door. Aunt Beth looked at her husband as he entered the kitchen and smiled; he was perspiring, but okay... Family members began entering the house. All six of their children were accounted for with their families. Other relatives and friends had also joined their crowd. Roo looked at the people entering the kitchen and wondered — where are we going...where is Uncle Benjamin taking us? Then he thought about his friend, Dr. Jones and hoped that he would be alright. "Okay, family," Uncle Ben announced, "let's head out; we're heading to a place of safety..."

Michael, Roo, and Michael's brother-in-law Kenneth, carried the crates to the automobiles. They placed one of the crates in the back of Uncle Benjamin's automobile and the other two in the back of Aunt Emily's automobile: her husband was standing outside the vehicle waiting. It was early in the morning, but still quite warm. Everyone present could smell smoke and hear gunfire. Uncle Benjamin was the last to leave the house. His son's watched him as he nodded his head and patted a budge at his waist. They knew that that meant he had his side-arm — in case of an "emergency." His head nod also indicated that he knew that they all had theirs at the ready... He instructed, "Family, friends, it's hot, but please keep your jackets and hats on — see that the little ones don't take theirs off: it's for their protection from the debris." He directed the drivers in the order they should follow one another. "Stay in this order — and flash you lights if there is any problem...any automobile ahead of the auto flashing their lights will also flash their lights until the lead car stops." He looked up into the night sky and said, "Please see us through..." He tucked his walking stick under his arm and joined his wife, Michael, Jo Ann, Roo, Kevin, Joe, and Lawrence, his youngest grandson, in his large car. Michael drove out to the street and turned toward Greenwood Avenue. Eleven cars followed. It was quite a motorcade. As they crossed the first intersection, the four remaining Author family members that had supported a crowd of Greenwood citizens earlier — Daniel, Albert, William, and Lee — saw the motorcade and jumped on the running boards of the slow moving vehicles. The men were a welcomed sight. Uncle Benjamin sat with an erect posture, with his wife Bethany in the center seat by his side.

Whites at Archer and Boston begin to push east down Archer toward Cincinnati in the face of fire from defenders. Heavy (gun) firing had begun at the Frisco Depot. Major Daley found a large group of Whites firing into the (Negro) area. He enlisted 20 volunteers to help contain the men in a triangular formation, from Boston to the end of the Frisco Platform at

Cincinnati, then back across the tracks. At daybreak, the loosely organized army of White rioters entered the (Negro) district in two movements. The first movement was a push from the south that came across the rail-yard, covered by White snipers. (The) push moved through the business district, and into the neighborhood: there was looting and burning. A second front of Whites attacked from the north down Standpipe Hill. They ran into, and through, crowds of (Negro) refugees who were fleeing from their homes. Whites in spotter planes oversaw the entire battle from above. With no official authority, the planes were used to locate pockets of (Negro) resistance for the White ground forces. Indeed, an "uncivil" civil war was fully engaged...

CHAPTER TEN

Wednesday

June 1ˢᵗ

"The Math After"

The booming thunder of social discord, upheaval, and violence in the district was resounding...

500 Whites around (the)Frisco Depot (were) fighting with several Blacks that were firing (guns) from housetops. General Barrett, the Adjutant General, and his troops left Oklahoma City on a special train (en route to Tulsa)to help quell the turmoil. Some where in the distant, a whistle (was) blown, and shooting took up all over town. People began shooting out of the Masons and Oddfellows hall, one man (was) shot from a window and hit the sidewalk. The

> shooting lasted not more than about a half hour.
> Six spotter planes were in the air, and armed
> Whites were moving into "Little Africa." Two
> thousand Blacks (were) fleeing town to the
> north.

The Author family drove the cars as far as they could on the side streets of the district before they were forced to abandon the vehicles and walk — the large debris was impassable. Like Lott, Abraham's nephew in the Old Testament, who gallantly led his family from the destruction of Sodom, Uncle Benjamin led his large familial group: Michael and Roo were "the warriors in the rear. Besides Uncle Benjamin, only Michael knew of the family's destination. This was to limit the chances of revealing the whereabouts of their safe haven; and in the event that Uncle Benjamin met his demise in his efforts to save the family. With every stride, the family's confidence grew — their leader, their patriarch, had determination and confidence written on his face.

> Everything on Archer from Boston east to Elgin (was) on
> fire. Between 8 & 9 a.m. the fire (was noticed). Almost
> the (entirety) of the west side of Greenwood and about
> half of the east side between Archer and Cameron were
> on fire. The Redwing was totally destroyed by fire.

Roo could see that they were approaching a corner that was familiar to him. They were near Dr. Jones' medical office. Dr. Jones had become dear to Roo — he had forged a great friendship with the doctor. Then, his mind suddenly took him to his family back in Georgia; they wouldn't believe what was happening to him in Tulsa...for that matter, no one would believe it. Indeed, Roo's family knew of the happenings in Tulsa — of course; his father

Joseph was a policeman and a member of the local NAACP; he was one of the first to get the news over the wire — "Racial Riot in Tulsa's Negro Quarter — STOP — Many feared injured and dead — STOP"...Unbeknown to Roo, his family was frantic with worry. They, like many others who heard the news, did the best thing they could — pray and attempt to call relatives in Tulsa. While the Negroes trusted that their prayers would get through; their phone calls didn't... When the static sounding voices of operators did finally answer their calls — "Number pleeez," the response was the same: "Sorry caller; all lines are disrupted..."

In the Greenwood District, Benjamin Author's family could hear the firing of guns nearby – while dogs could be heard barking wildly in the distance. Above them, in the windows of a few apartment buildings, they could hear the crying of children and babies...their community was collapsing down around them, their world seemed to be coming to an end. As they came to the Greenwood Avenue intersection, the group stopped. Roo noticed that the men and women in the *pack* began looking over the shoulders of those ahead of them in an attempt to see the purpose of the pause. Some noticed a dismal expression on their leader's face as he took in the sight before him. (Leaders are always the first to see what lay ahead....) It wasn't the sound of gunfire, the overhead planes, or the yelling of racial obscenities that caused Uncle Benjamin to pause; but the horrific destruction of the community he had helped to build and cultivate. There was debris everywhere — glass, broken light bulbs, bricks, clothing, torn children's toys, and burned out automobiles.

Now, the group again moved forward as the men in the front near Uncle Benjamin, in a motion reminiscent of Moses being assisted with the *raising* of his staff by his Hebrew helpers during battle, placed their hands on his

shoulders and steadied the walking stick that was in his right hand. The group
slowly rounded the corner onto Greenwood Avenue. This area of the district
appeared to be worse off than the area they had just left. Weren't they moving
into harms way rather than away from it, Roo thought? Howbeit, this was
their course. Again, the family had come to depend and rely on Uncle
Benjamin's wisdom and guidance — at this point it was paramount.

Yes, he was right, Roo had his bearings right. They were near Dr. Jones'
office. Oh no, and there was Dr. Jones on his knees attending to a young
patient on the sidewalk in front of his office. A few of the men in the family
ran ahead of Uncle Benjamin to aid the young girl on whom Dr. Jones was
working. A large sign had fallen from the top of the building and landed on
the girl and her family as they had attempted to evacuate the area. A mound
of bricks from the building had subsequently landed on the top of the sign.
Dr. Jones had used his professional sense of triage, attending to the young girl
who was trapped under the sign and bricks near her waist. The rest of the
family perished under its full weight. Dr. Jones had witnessed the sight from
his broken office window as he attempted to quickly gather bandages and
medicine for what he knew would be necessary, given this emergent situation.
He didn't know of his medical partner's whereabouts, but knew that he had
to go into action: for the community. The men attempted to move the large
bricks, which ironically had served as material for a building which
represented health and physical wellness, a medical office; but now had
caused the injury and death of those under it...

Around the corner, the sound of an angry mob could be heard approaching
in their direction. Heads in the group turned toward the approaching angry
voices. On the other side of the neighborhood, they heard the sound of
explosives and witnessed a cloud of smoke billowing into the air. Dr. Jones

looked up at Uncle Benjamin. The two men, by virtue of a shared intense stare communicated: carry on with the plan. They were "Tulsa Material." Uncle Benjamin led the group, rapidly now, down the block toward his financial office. The doctor now attempted to use his energy to help move the sign off the young girl. When all attempts failed, he urged the remaining Author men to catch up with their family — he would stay to attend to the young surviving victim. The mob was near and the men, hard-pressed to leave the girl and Dr. Jones, reluctantly moved down the mangled avenue to catch Uncle Benjamin and the rest of the family — they had failed the young girl and Dr. Jones. Dr. Jones had given them no other recourse but to retreat from their efforts to aid the girl; the doctor's intentionally loud voice prompted them to comply as not to draw the attention of the approaching White mob to their fleeing family members — only a few yards ahead... Roo, still in the back of the group with his cousin Michael, kept his eyes pealed toward Dr. Jones while holding onto Michael's right shoulder for guidance — he occasionally tripped over debris in the street. He saw his relatives racing toward them: they couldn't budge the material which trapped the young girl before the mob's arrival. Roo's eyes got wide as he could make out Dr. Jones on his knees looking up toward the mob leaders. Dr. Jones appeared to be communicating with the men before hunkering over the young girl. Roo saw three flashes over Dr. Jones' back; it seemed to happen in slow motion. Everyone in the group heard the gunfire. Roo collapsed to the ground...not from tripping over debris but from the anguish of the gruesome sight. Dr. Jones had been mortally wounded. Michael stopped and helped Roo to his feet. Both young men had tears in their eyes. They pushed up against the backs of those ahead of them. The mob was moving — they were loud. Uncle Benjamin, still leading the group, knew what the gun shots behind him meant — his friend was gone. He shook his head as if shuttering, and increased the pace forward — his office was now in sight. He handed the keys to one of his nephews at his side, who ran ahead to open the office doors. They had arrived. For the moment, everything was intact.

Uncle Benjamin allowed his wife, Aunt Beth, to enter ahead of him. The other women followed, and then the men. Strangely, it appeared that Uncle Benjamin had planned for the emergency. As things at the Tulsa police station had deteriorated, the calls were made: the right number of cars were available and, once on foot, the women were positioned in the middle of the group with the younger children. The men were assigned to circle them. Roo and Michael were the back of the protection ring. Like the U.S. Calvary retreating an overwhelming attack and closing the giant, wooden gates of their fort behind them, the last Author family member and friends had made it inside as the elegant doors were closed and a metal gate drawn. Once closed, the gate formed a myriad of diamond-shaped openings. Finally, they were all safe in the plush office of Author Financial.

More explosions could be heard outside — it seemed to get closer. The power was off and the men lit lanterns; they pulled the shades down. Michael took Roo to the room that was not included on his first tour of the office on the day that he had arrived in Tulsa. Roo was amazed. The heavy, vault-like doors opened to a room that had multiple supplies, and first aid containers. "Over there," Michael said. He directed Roo's attention to the additional lanterns needed in the office area. There appeared to be at least two dozen, each with a supply of kerosene. "Wow," Roo exclaimed, as he noticed additional containers of kerosene. Uncle Benjamin determined that these supplies would probably be the first needed as they entered the office — first aid supplies for the injured, lights and blankets. Michael said, "There's water and food downstairs in the basement — there's also 30 cots down there. There's enough space for 50 people or more. Dad even set up a make-shift kitchen..." For now, it seemed that everyone was safe in the main office area, no need to head downstairs.

Ms. Lottie was also in the office with the family. She had assisted Uncle Benjamin in amassing his emergency food supplies. Given the size of the group, they could survive for a period of 10 days. Uncle Benjamin cautioned everyone to speak quietly at all times and directed them to a whistle — now around his neck. "If and when I blow this whistle, you must walk to the door over there," he pointed to the storage room, "and proceed down the stairs. There will be no time for questions and answers at that point, just move...women and children will head down first and then the men." As he spoke, Uncle Benjamin had some of the men in the family posted at each corner of the office where there were windows. There was an eruption of gunfire down the street. Uncle Benjamin hesitated and then disappeared into his personal office with three of Roo's cousins. They returned with military riffles. Roo thought, what had led Uncle Benjamin to the point of these preparations and measures? How did he predict this event? So far, everything seemed to be in order during this period of disorder... however, someone was missing — Dr. Jones. He was also to be included in the group during this state of emergency. Dr. Jones was sorely missed.

Suddenly, there was a banging at the front door. Then pounding... The pounding continued for several minutes. Everyone in the room stared at Uncle Benjamin. He raised his right index finger and without a word pointed to the storage room. Everyone began to move swiftly in the direction of his pointing finger. Roo, Michael, and Uncle Benjamin could hear a heavy voice outside the door: "I know I saw them go in here; there must be a hundred niggers in this fancy jungle. What are we waiting for, let's go in..." They began breaking the windows of the door and attempted to reach in to unlock it. Everyone — except for Roo, Michael, and Uncle Benjamin — had entered the storage area and descended the stairs. Instantly, Uncle Benjamin concluded that if they could all reach the storage room and close the vault door, without any noise, perhaps they'll enter the office and conclude that no one was actually there — no need for further pursuit. Within minutes, the three were behind the vault door as Uncle Benjamin locked it from the inside. He prayed and then turned, grabbed an additional lantern and followed behind his son Michael to the waiting group in the basement. Again, they were safe. If their pursuers successfully entered the office, Uncle Benjamin was sure they would not be able to breach the vault door.

Many of the woman and children were already sitting on the unfolded cots. Thankfully, the depth and thick walls of the basement blocked out the sound of gunfire and explosions — the children could sleep. Aunt Beth and Ms. Lottie were serving coffee and tea to those who accepted. They thought that a hot beverage would help calm their nerves. Uncle Benjamin periodically sent Michael and one of his brothers to the vault door ... during their latest check, they were able to detect the forced entry into their father's office — the mob had made their way in. They had breached both the doors and the metal gates. Michael and his brother took turns looking through a peek hole that their father had drilled through one of the walls. They could see the movement of men in the office. Although they couldn't quite see everything that was going on in the office through the glass, they could see that the office was now in complete disarray. Michael noticed that the tall plants that had separated his desk from the receptionist area had been pulled out of their pots. It appeared that there was dirt and mud on the floor and rugs. Some of the men were standing with their arms crossed over their chest with cigars in their mouths as others could be seen hauling some of the furniture pass the destroyed office doors. Michael could feel his blood boiling. Just then, the peek glass was blocked by dark material. At first, Michael couldn't tell what was blocking his view. Had one of them discovered the peek glass? Were they attempting to look in? No, he finally realized that the picture that hung just above the peek glass on the other side of the wall was being viewed by the person. He finally witnessed a portly White man abruptly back away from the peek glass as he ripped the painting down — his derby-style hat fell to the floor during the abrupt move. The edge of the ripped painting, now, partly blocked Michael's view. The portly man's backside was visible as he turned and reached down to recover his hat from the littered floor. Michael nearly pointed the barrel of the riffle in the peek hole to fire a few rounds — he was sure he could pick off at least one of them... "It's alright," his older brother assured him in a whispered tone, "God sees all and knows all." More importantly, it appeared that the mob had discontinued their search for the family. Uncle Benjamin, having later received the report from his two sons while sitting in the basement, concluded that the White men had stopped their search, for one, because they probably couldn't find any evidence of the family having been in the office, and the distraction of "scavenging" the office for the wealth of its goodly materials... Michael didn't share everything with his dad; having worked in the office for a few years and his work-related visits downtown, he was able to identify a couple of the White men through the peek glass. He was enraged, but kept it to himself for now. His fiancée, also part of the hidden group, came to his side and grabbed him by the waist. She offered him a kiss on the cheek and then staying near, placed her head on his shoulders. Perhaps, the worst was behind them. For now, Benjamin

Author decided that they would all stay put. Roo, sitting in a corner and not privy to the detailed happenings at the courthouse in downtown Tulsa, suddenly heard the booming voice of the visiting minister replayed in his head: "Deacon Author," the minister had addressed Uncle Ben, "Jonah's disobedience to God caused the stormy weather that struck that ship as he attempted to escape his charge in Nineveh; Jonah knew it... and finally instructed the sailors to hoist him overboard to save the ship...the sea calmed down afterwards..." Roo considered that if he was the cause of this social tempest as a result of his forbidden meeting with Vickie Herd, maybe he should be "hoisted" and sacrificed... to relieve the pain on his family members and their community — enough damage and death had already taken place...

Uncle Benjamin Author sat in one of the wooden chairs with his walking stick between his inter-digited fingers and crossed thumbs. They were now in the "waiting game" phase of their survival mission. Movement out of their place of safety, too soon, could spell disaster and bring the long-time planning and developmental efforts of the grand gentleman to naught...here, patience was key. Aunt Beth approached Uncle Benjamin with a cup of coffee, kissed the top of his head, and said, "Ben, you're something...you've always been a good husband, father, and leader." Your intelligence, observation, and sensitivity to our Lord has preserved our lives and now allows 'our stories' to continue." Roo watched his uncle and aunt with great admiration. He looked back at his other relatives — all safe and sound — and thought on a comment his father had made to him one day as he rode in their automobile: "The mark of success is the wellbeing of those you teach, support, and guide..." Roo marveled; as impressed as he was with his uncle's financial office upstairs, he was now even more impressed with his uncle's ingenuity and foresight. The space in which they owed their safety and well-being was remarkable. "Uncle

Benjamin," Roo asked in a voice of great curiosity, "how did you know that this would happen? What were the signs?" Everyone in the room stopped talking. It was the question of the hour — maybe for the ages... They wanted to take in the words and wonderful wisdom of the man who had led them to safety. Uncle Benjamin started... "I had a vision; an ongoing vision. Although I couldn't always understand the meaning of the vision, I began pulling things together...it was a though I was moving, behaving, acting without a clear and concise motive. God instructed Noah to build an Ark on dry land; and I was led to construct a shelter in the center of our sheltered Greenwood community..." Roo was mesmerized. As his uncle told of his visions, He began reflecting upon his dreams — the dreams that seemed to have a troubling theme was THIS — the "Tulsa Riots" — the culmination of his dream story. It seemed to fit. He remembered the buildings, the faces, the tears... Uncle Benjamin interrupted his thoughts: "Of course, I didn't know exactly when it would happen, but I knew it would... Roo, if I had known that it would happen now, I would have stopped you from coming here..."

> The fighting came to a stop when martial law was declared. The Black district, after five to six hours of battle and looting, was a mass of black clouds of smoke rolling above the ruins of thirty-some city blocks of rubble and ashes. The armory began to house the (Negro) wounded. (Major) Brown began treating the Black wounded at the armory.

It was time to leave the lair. First would be the men with their riffles. They were directed toward the vault door. Michael's brother, Sam, opened the door. They moved out of the storage room area into the now decimated office. It was completely and totally ransacked. Furniture had been removed, pictures damaged, and the floors severely mangled... the grandfather clock was kicked over on its side...even the bear rug in Uncle Ben's office was slashed to threads. Suddenly, Aunt Beth called out, "Ben, come over here...look." Uncle Benjamin moved toward his wife. Everyone began to assemble near their patriarch and matriarch. It was amazing; beyond reason, in the midst of the utter destruction of his office, the portrait of Uncle Benjamin was untouched, it had been preserved — not a scratch. During this period of heaviness, this was a reason to smile. Indeed, everyone in the group — from the youngest to the oldest — began to smile...

Everyone now turned their attention to the front. They all looked past the doors, now hanging off their hinges. The metal gates; which probably impeded and slowed the intruders entry into the office, was, indeed, cut through. Against Uncle Benjamin's better (and now highly revered) judgment, Aunt Beth was the first to reach and walk through the opening — they could see Ms. Lottie's damaged restaurant across the street. Ms. Lottie only sighed and tilted her head to the side. The group stood outside on the landing. There was a collective sense of having been violated — a kin to returning to one's home and finding that it has been breached; burglarized and touched by filthy hands. The group noticed garments, family photos, baby pictures, kitchen utensils, chairs, Christmas decorations and even a black doctor's bag, strewn across the great thoroughfare of Greenwood Avenue. The thought was of the unruly crowds of Whites as well as those who came to 'spectate', taking advantage of the horrid situation; entering the home of another — the home of those they had earlier refused to enter by kinder means... Gawking, peeking; touching those things that those who resided therein considered precious... Angry hands always seek to tear down.

Observing from the top step, along-side the family, Roo considered the desolation; the quietness of the scene. The once busy street was completely deserted. This was the moon... or at least the moon as he imagined it. A place devoid of activity and life — maybe a place of **past lives**... Why did Vickie even think that the moon would be the optimal place for a wonderful, lively relationship? Maybe it was just the sense of solitude she had considered. Then he thought: Vickie, oh yeah, Vickie, she may have been the cause of all of this!

As Aunt Beth stood surveying the sight before her, her three daughters, Michael's sisters, gathered together to her left - they kept a close eye on their mother... Korrine, who was standing in the middle, simultaneously squeezed the hands of Katherine on her right and Kellene on her left. They empathized with their beloved mother as she reached for Ms. Lottie... Aunt Beth held Ms. Lottie around her shoulders while facing the debris-strewn street, and began humming the tune of "God Bless America"... With tears now streaming down her cheeks, she stopped humming and spoke the final words of the song: "Our home," she paused as though taking it all in, and then continued with the evidence of some great inner-force, "sweet, home..."

CHAPTER ELEVEN

"The long Journey Home"

The epic in Roo's lap: Roo was writing voraciously in his journal. He had
survived the nation's worst and deadliest "race war." The once-thriving
community of the Greenwood District was virtually decimated. Where
buildings survived the devastation, spirits and souls had collapsed. An epic
story was coming into being in Roo's lap. Roo, traveled west to Tulsa as a
man in waiting... now he was returning to Georgia as a bona fide man — after
all, Roo's father always said, "It's not your biology that makes you a man, it's
managing life's tough situations and experiences that make you a man." In
many ways, this time of reflection, beyond the horrible event in Tulsa, was a
turning point for Roo. It was at this juncture that Roo changed his focus
from numbers to letters. He had once determined that he would become a
financial professional, like his Uncle Benjamin, but now he realized the

importance of history. He felt empowered to tell a story — a story for the ages.

Traveling eastward on the speeding train to Georgia, he paused to think of his kin folks back in Tulsa; there in the midst of the horrible ruins of the Greenwood District. Of course, he was grateful to God for preserving the lives of his relatives: Uncle Benjamin, Aunt Beth, Michael, and the others; but he felt that he had abandoned them in their darkest hour. Uncle Benjamin forced him to leave for his own safety and well being. He assured the young man that they would be just fine. Uncle Benjamin exclaimed, "Our God and inner-strength will see us through." Roo's grimace turned into a smile as he remembered his uncle's last statement as he ushered Roo to his seat on the train: "It was great men and women that built this district. Once a man learns to build, he can always build — he never forgets how to build... a carpenter is always a carpenter..."

Again, seated near the inter-car door of the Negro train car, Roo stopped writing and closed his eyes. As he concentrated on his Uncle's last words to him before his train's departure — "carpenter" — he heard a knock at the window of the train's door. Sakes alive — he couldn't believe his eyes: it was Vickie Herd expressing a bright, dimpled smile. She was staring intently at Roo... She was also a passenger on the east-bound train...

"What is Vickie doing on the train? Is she following me? Is she attempting to escape the menagerie in Tulsa? Is her family on the train? Is she *leading the authorities to me?* His heart rate increased... he begin to lose his breath.

Roo expected to see two burly, White policemen burst in from behind Vickie waving their 'billy clubs' — prepared to take him into custody…

…Indeed, they did! One policeman appeared from behind and promptly step ahead of Vickie, virtually pushing her over with his broad shoulders, while the second rotund police man entered and stopped at Vickie's side. He reached over and held her left shoulder firmly while he looked toward Roo and grimaced. Roo was overtaken with fear and anxiety — he knew better then to put up a struggle with the law men. The first policeman's face was red with fury as he abruptly bent toward Roo's face, with his billy club in hand, and yelled, "Boy, yer under arrest for the assault and mishandling of this young White girl, and for the death of many of our citizens back in Tulsa…Darkie, we finally got you. You'll pay dearly for yer dreadful deeds…" The policeman raised his club above his head and swung it hard toward Roo's head. Roo cringed as he expected instant impact…The billy club never reached his head. The police weapon, and its handler disappeared; they weren't actually there…they were a figment of Roo's wild imagination — but Vickie **was there** *at the glass door; staring at Roo…*

Roo's heart continued to beat at a rapid pace. No policemen, he thought. Are they going to burst through the door? He tracked the passage of time by the thumping heart beats that now seemed to be amplified in his ears…20 beats….25 beats….40 beats…60. Still, only Vickie at the door. Whew, it's — it's okay. These thoughts quickly raced through Roo's mind like the speeding locomotive on which they were now traveling… Although he was anxious and puzzled, he was also strangely glad to see her. He hadn't spoken to her since their meeting on Sunday night behind the downtown buildings. He yearned to run to her and embrace her. He wanted to lift her off the ground and carry her to a far off, unbiased, nonjudgmental land… a place where Negroes and Whites could truly engage in an unrestricted, unfettered, limitless "relationship." Vickie had his attention and waited for a response — she was standing between the two train cars: Whites-only and Negro. Roo noticed that the inter-train door of the Whites-only car had the curtain drawn behind her — no peering White eyes, he thought. He looked around and over his shoulder to inspect his passenger car for any observing Negroes. He thought: Vickie had earlier shown a quality of being bold and unabashed; why didn't she just barge into the Negro car? He was actually glad she didn't. A brief bit of anger begin to rise in him as he thought about her domineering posture back in downtown Tulsa. He had also considered her to be the possible source of the race riots in Tulsa... But, now, standing in his view, Vickie was so pretty. With a sense of trepidation, he cautiously pointed to his pocket watch, which he had pulled out and held up his hand with his fingers fanned open. He then pointed down toward Vickie's elegant purple shoes. Vickie realized that Roo's signal meant: Meet me between the cars — where you are now standing, in five minutes. In the meantime, Roo would attempt to cleverly and inconspicuously close the "Negro" door curtains for privacy. Roo also kept in mind that he would have to watch the time for scheduled employee car-to-car passage — it was getting close to lunch.

Right on time: they met in the small space behind the cloak of the inter-car "curtains." Vickie instantly grabbed Roo around the neck and kissed his lips — he wasn't going to get away this time... their lips were locked for twenty seconds. Roo extended his arms and braced himself against the two inter-car door sections that separated the cars — he was careful not to cause a bump or thud against the doors. Vickie's lips and mouth tasted like peppermint. By the time he identified the flavor, he felt a hard piece of peppermint candy being forced into his mouth... from her mouth. His closed eyes popped open just as she slowly opened her eyes and began blinking. Her blue eyes, up-close, were unfathomable. She had exchanged oral fluids with him... They stopped and stared at one another. Licking her lips, Vickie broke the silence: "The ancient Greeks and Romans considered peppermint an aphrodisiac." With his lips covered with Vickie's lip stick and her peppermint candy in his mouth, he stood still; Roo couldn't speak...

Roo's mind catapulted him back to the issue of "power differentials." He realized that his and Vickie's relationship — on any level — would be dynamic, to say the least. In society, Vickie had a colossal amount of power. However, Roo was adjusting to the power he had in their relationship. Indeed, he held a substantial amount of power. Part of his power was keeping hers in check. Coupling his past conversation with Mr. Smithson, the banker, with his recent "Vickie-related" experiences: he came to realize that despite the perceptions and attitudes, power should not be arbitrarily given away, but simply recognized and dealt with. He considered the passionate kiss from Vickie. While her power led her to kiss him without permission — he knew he had the power to limit the use of *her* power — didn't he? She was not automatically afforded all the power — was she? He began to realize that in any given situation power can be used, preferably; or given to others — which typically happened... most people used it as a barrier to their own actions: to limit themselves. He concluded that this often ended in helplessness and hopelessness... Uh; at this minute, Roo's thoughts had spun out of control — he was confused...maybe at this point, Vickie's power over his mind, prevailed.

Vickie, realizing that Roo was not aware of the reports back in Tulsa, said, "Roo, I'm so sorry about what happen to the Greenwood District. The folks there didn't deserve it. When I heard about it, I was just sick. I thought that I had lost you forever. I also thought of the many people I had met in

Greenwood through my father. Roo, I don't know what I would have done if you were hurt. How are your relatives; did they survive the incident?" Roo was a little put off with the word "incident." "Yes, they're fine." Roo said, "I was concerned that our interactions Sunday night might have caused a problem in both our communities," he paused — "if someone found out..." Vickie shot back: "Roo, our relationship had nothing at all to do with what happened in Tulsa. My dad told me that it started in downtown when a Negro man, Dick Rowland, assaulted a white girl, Sarah Page, in the Drexel Building. The girl screamed and a clerk, who was at Renberg's after hours, ran to her aid." Vickie finished, "Roo, it's the way things operate for better or worse... I'm sorely saddened by the events — and I definitely believe that there is more to the story than I just shared with you." Roo was strangely relieved to hear the report. Roo thought: Vickie considers it an "incident" — I consider it a riot; a major event...

Vickie, in addition, reported: "I'm on my way to college." (She had been a grade ahead of Roo.) "My parents thought that this would be a good time to leave Tulsa, given the recent incident, to settle in with my relatives during the summer." Roo cocked his head to the side.

Roo was still facing Vickie when he detected a change in the train's wheel-to-rail noise. The clicking noise became more rapid and louder. A second later, the train bobbed and shifted making them both lose their balance. In an instant, Vickie fell back against the cushioned panel behind her. Roo's well-conditioned body was pressed hard against her. Vickie, who exhaled as his body struck hers, suddenly felt a sense of exhilaration. She loved the presence of Roo's masculine body against hers. Vickie quickly locked her arms around his slender waist and kept him close. Roo attempted to brace himself against the cushion at her back — reaching on either side of her. Roo was moved… and Vickie felt the "movement." Suddenly, he caught sight of movement to his left; from the Negro car door. Vickie looked up at Roo's face and said, "Roo, honey, you're perspiring…" She unabashedly and with a display of great comfort reached her hand to his face and wiped the sweat from his forehead. She reached behind his neck and found more perspiration. Vickie, still holding him with the other arm, finally allowed him to separate from their adjacent position. His shirt was moist with sweat. The form of his well-developed, 'shirt-shrouded', chest was again visible to her as when they had first met in downtown Tulsa. She finally looked over to see what Roo had noticed. It was the face of a little Negro girl, behind a respiration-vapor, smudged window giggling at the sight of Roo and Vickie. Roo wondered: how long has she been standing there at the window? Is she old enough to report what she just saw? WILL HER MOTHER PULL THE CURTAIN OPEN ANY MINUTE TO FIND THE LITTLE GIRL — VICKIE — ME? Roo craned his neck and aggressively kissed Vickie on the lips. He quickly told her to meet him after dinner. Roo said to Vickie before opening the door where the child was standing, "Same *place*; same pretty *face*…" Vickie began to blush again. She tilted her head to the side, bit her lip and then smiled. The dimples Roo remembered the first time he had met her appeared once again. As Roo stepped into the Negro car to pick the girl up, Vickie reached over and tickled Roo's side. He looked back and beamed a bright smile in her direction. The door slowly closed behind him.

What are the chances, he thought, as he stepped past the drawn curtains of the Negro passenger car. Roo had dodged another bullet. He felt almost invincible. Everything was calm and quiet in the car. The mother of the child

Roo had in his arms hadn't even noticed the absence of her daughter. Roo placed the little girl by her mother's side, as the mother said, "Girl — don't you wonder away from me again..." Then looking at Roo sheepishly, said, "Thank you, young man." Roo nodded his head with a smile then turned back to notice a large White conductor entering the car passed the curtain he had just darted through after his meeting with Vickie. He thought: That was close — thank you little girl... He went back to his seat and flopped down. He smiled to himself and considered a statement made by Uncle Benjamin at the family dinner in Tulsa: "If you cross the line, they will follow you back..." In his mind, Vickie had followed.

The speeding locomotive headed in a southeastward direction at a seemingly furious pace. Roo noticed the leaves of the trees along the track wave in the whisk of the train-produced air current. Lunch had been served and the trays collected an hour earlier. The ham sandwich with sharp cheddar cheese, mayonnaise and tomatoes, with a side of coleslaw and tomato soup, was filling. The sharp cheese seemed to linger on his palate.

It seemed that Roo was reliving "his" story in reverse order as the train returned to the venues and settings that he witnessed and observed on the Tulsa, Oklahoma route. Yes, a return to the same panoramic stories — however, the **context** seemed profoundly different. For one, this part of Roo's adventurous story now included the salient character of Victoria Herd — a person who, for all intents and purposes, and from an outsider's perspective, had totally nothing in common with him other than the fact that she was moving in the same direction, at the same speed, on the same vehicle. Of course, the differences and things that were uncommon between them were multitudinous — for one, she was seated in a car that was designated for "Whites only." Roo determined that it seemed that all his short life there was always more of a focus and effort to emphasize and bolster the differences between Negroes and Whites rather than the similarities they shared. How exhausting, Roo thought... You're different: you sit on this bench and reserve the other for Whites. You're not like us: you use this fountain and leave this other one for White folks. You're a Negro: you attend this school and leave Whites alone in their schools. A porter from behind called out... "Coffee, tea, soda water; coffee, tea, soda water..." The anxiety of the recent event in Tulsa seemed to gradually melt away. However, Roo didn't necessarily think that this was a good thing: it felt as though he was now emotionally abandoning his Tulsa relatives and their community. The porter was now standing at the side of his seat looking down at him with a calming smile. "Young, sir, would you like a soda-pop?" Roo nodded and said, "Yes, Sir," and presented the porter with a single coin and accepted the refreshment. The seat across from Roo was vacant on his home-bound journey; however, he could visualize Dr. Jones in the seat. In his vision, Dr. Jones looked at him — his posture was quite erect and his forehead furrowed with wrinkled ridges. His facial expression seemed uncharacteristically, undefined. In Roo's mind, the vision of Dr. Jones' face almost gave the appearance of ambiguity. Roo had known Dr. Jones' statements and expression to communicate direction and assurance; but now it seemed his vision of Dr. Jones projected uncertainty and doubt. Roo felt unsettled in his spirit. Roo thought, oh no, first it was a dream now a vision... Roo reached for his journal — he had plenty to recount. It was now 1:30 PM.

The locomotive seemed to slow down. Roo heard the locomotive's horn blow loud and clear. The train was pulling into a medium-sized station.

According to the train schedule, this was a refueling station. This meant that the train would remain at the platform for 45 minutes to take on more food and supplies as well as more passengers. Roo had decided to stay on the train and write. However, as he glanced out the window, he saw Vickie standing outside the train, staring in his direction. She dropped a lipstick canister on the platform and bent over — facing in his direction — to recover it. Roo noticed that her shoulder strap slid down her shoulder as she reached for the lipstick holder. Her white undergarment strap was visible. She suddenly looked up in the direction of Roo's window and winked. Dimples formed in her cheeks. Roo noticed that she had her feet positioned in a quaint and slightly pigeon-toed slant. It made her look even more elegant and feminine in Roo's mind. Vickie somehow knew that Roo would be looking; she was right. Vickie recovered the lipstick holder and walked toward the edge of the platform, away from the animation of the crowd. She looked over her shoulder at Roo, who was still watching, before stepping down, what appeared to be, a deserted stairway. Roo placed his journal under his seat and made sure his reservation stub was in place. He grabbed his suit jacket and proceeded to the train's exit. He noticed that other Negroes were socializing on the opposite end of the train station's platform. Of course, his proclivity was to head in the direction of the Negro section, but he quickly placed his flat-cap on his head, raised the collar of his jacket, placed his hands in his pockets and walked toward the edge of the platform where he had last spotted Vickie. No one seemed to notice him as he casually looked back over his shoulder at the train and passengers on the platform. It all seemed too easy. How could it be? Vickie was a beautiful White girl. How could she move anywhere in public without being observed; if not by other women, certainly by young men. Dr. Jones' vision came to Roo's mind — the vision with the unclear expression. Roo thought, maybe I'm now at a point in my life where I am developing and creating "my own" destiny. I'm now a man; I can't blame anyone for my actions or their consequences. As he had shared with his family earlier, his journey to manhood would be lonely.

He could her Vickie's voice in the distant calling: "Roo, Roo, is that you up there? Come down, there's nobody around..." Roo could feel his heart beating in his chest. It almost felt as if it would soon be visible in his mouth. Before he knew it, he was descending down a few steps along side the train station. He could hear Vickie's voice: "Ah, there you are sweetie, I could hardly eat lunch thinking of you... I longed to hug you and squeeze you." Roo did not resist as she grabbed his head, near his ears and pulled his lips to hers. It seemed that she wouldn't let him go. Her lips tasted like peppermint — again. He raised his head in an attempt to break the seal between their lips, but Vickie persisted as she raised the weight of her body to her tippy-toes. She finally broke the lip seal... They were *alone* in the shadow of the train station. "Roo said, "Wow, it's hot — it must be a hundred degrees here." He continued, "How did you know about this area?" "I know a lot, fella... I can't tell you all my secrets," Vickie responded. Roo didn't press the issue. Vickie said, "Roo, I wish I could ride in the train car with you. I would love to sit next to you and hold your hand: touch you in public. It's funny, back in Tulsa, we talked about riding a train together... I think I said, to the moon. There are no tracks in that direction, but I wish we could go somewhere where you could be seen for the man you truly are and not the 'Negro man' society tries to limit you to." Roo was speechless. They could hear soft music in the background. Vickie, moved her hand and arms under and past Roo's arms. She placed them on his muscular back; just under his shoulder blades while wedging her right leg between his legs. Ipso facto, Vickie had her feet on each side of Roo's right foot. She was aggressive. For Vickie, the physical effort paid off, their bodies pressed close together — her pelvis against the quadriceps of his thigh, she began leading Roo in a slow dance in the shadows. They moved in a circular motion, then backwards and forwards. Their moves were smooth; rhythmic. It seemed almost rehearsed. Pressed close to Roo's leg, Vickie audibly exhaled as she felt the inter-play of his thigh muscles contract and relax, contract and relax, contract and relax... Roo could vicariously feel Vickie's abdomen engage it's physiological inward, outward motion as she seemed to periodically hold her breath — then release. Roo, against the tenacious strength of his inhibitions — crying out in his head: don't do it, stop; slowly and simultaneously removed his hands from his pockets and placed them on Vickie's shapely waist and then slowly moved them down to her hips. He could feel evidence of her lower undergarments through her dress... The crossroads had been crossed. In the past, his experience of interacting with Vickie's person was by happenstance, as a result of Vickie's willful explorations; but now it was due to his own volitional exploits. He closed his eyes and closed out the world. For now, it was just him and Vickie — dancing at the station. A hot breeze rushed passed them. It only served to add to the heat of Vickie's passion for Roo. She had hoped that it would never end; but begin, over and over again. Roo's "biology," again, came to life. Instantly, Vickie looked up at Roo and smiled with a rose-colored face. He didn't notice her gaze. Vickie threw her head back, flared her nostrils, and closed her eyes as her Cloche hat fell to the ground. Roo finally opened his eyes and looked upward toward the partly cloudy sky and then upon Vickie's beautifully-flushed face. Soon, Vickie opened her eye lids and displayed her brilliant blue eyes. Indeed, whatever course this relationship took, Roo realized that he would take responsibility for the outcome — or its consequences. That's what men do. For all his experiences and all the wise counsel from relatives and friends; this was extraordinary. No one that he knew had had an inter-racial, romantic relationship. No role-model, no example from which to glean information. Not even his grandfather, John, could speak to it, except to perhaps say: "Don't do it. Don't even think of it." Indeed, before his visit to Tulsa, he hadn't. It was the furthest thing from his mind until he met Dr. Herd's pretty daughter: Victoria. Vickie broke the sensuous silence: "Randolph, maybe we could leave the country; perhaps Europe would be a more favorable place for us. This jarred Roo — this, the United States, was the only place he knew. Racism was a way of life — the only *life* he knew. But, maybe a new world, a life with Vickie would be worth the move...suddenly, from the top of the stairs they heard heavy foot steps approaching — there was no time to flee. They stopped moving. They "froze" — in the middle of the scorching summer heat.

The train station agent was at the top of the stairway looking down at the young couple. "Hey, you kids down there; what are you doing?" With a stern voice of concern he bellowed, "Young man, what are you doing with that girl?" He started down the stairs toward them. Roo could feel his knees begin to buckle. Vickie realized that they were still in the shadow of the train station; Roo's back was toward the approaching man. Roo tucked his hands back in his pockets and the collar of his suit jacket was still raised. Ah, Vickie thought — the agent didn't yet realize that she was with a Negro boy. Roo's caramel skin was concealed. As the agent reached the last step and approached them, Vickie called to him, "Sir, please don't come any closer — you'll embarrass me... My boyfriend and I are saying good bye before the train departs and I don't want you to see me in my, well, indecent state." The agent stopped. His face was flushed. He was sensitive to Vickie's appeal. He couldn't help but wink at Vickie who was looking around Roo's left shoulder. With a more distinct Irish accent, the agent called to Roo: "Sonny boy, you be careful with the pretty lass," he paused and then instructed, "and take off that jacket before you boil..." The agent then turned and ascended the stairs back to the platform.

Sweat on his brow, Roo pulled out his pocket watch and noticed that forty minutes had passed since their exit from the train. They had only five minutes to inconspicuously get back to the platform and on the train without suspicion. They heard the announcement. "All aboard — train 333 preparing to depart the station...All aboard!" Vickie knew just what to do to get them back on the train and preserve her "man" and their relationship. She would head around the corner to the train station's front entrance while Roo headed back up the steps. Their appearance on the station platform would be inconspicuously separate: Roo coming from the corner of the building and Vickie from inside the train station. Once Roo reached the platform, he stopped and stooped down to brush off his shoes as though removing dust and dirt. This allowed Victoria to embark on the train first. She stepped on the first train step and looked back at Roo as he remained in a stooped position. Even after her profound and pleasing interfacing, Vickie found her desire for Roo Author insatiable. The conductor looked at the pretty girl and then in the direction of her focus — toward Roo. He displayed an expression of mild disgust and instructed, "Please take your seat." She disappeared from sight.

Vickie headed toward her seat on the opposite side of the car, away from the platform. Noticing an empty seat near the platform-side window of the car, she stopped and decided to take one more look at Randolph on the platform. She began to feel "heat" radiating from her face. She was flush, she was miffed, no, angry; she was: jealous...Roo had just stood up to run to the train when three tall and shapely Negro teenage girls "delicately," blocked his path to the train. Roo hadn't noticed their presence until he stood up. All three girls were staring at him as though inspecting a new and highly desired garment. Roo looked past the girls to the train. The conductor looked at Roo with a cross expression and waved his arm abruptly beckoning him to the train. Two of the girls grabbed Roo's arms, one on Roo's left side and the other on his right, in a gesture to hold him close. The third girl, still in front of Roo, stepped toward him and gently brushing up against him whispered something in his left ear. The message made Roo simultaneously smile and blush... Vickie was now wildly jealous and had intentions on going back to the platform to claim *her* guy: she didn't care who observed. Before she could reach the door of the passenger car to intervene, Roo had politely pulled his arms free of the adoring females and gracefully squeezed pass the young lady in front of him and the one to his left. The two girls who held his arms still had their hands cupped in the form of Roo's biceps... the young lady who stood before him had the pleasure of feeling Roo's ample chest as he brushed pass her. The girls stood and gazed at Roo from behind as he ran to catch his train. Their eyes followed his every stride before he leapt on the train's step and disappeared... one of the girls brashly called after him causing heads to turn: "See ya, good-lookin'..." They looked at one another and giggled...

Safely on board the train, Roo thought, no one seems to be the wiser. It worked; but for how long? The conductor leaned out the door and waved his hand to the engineer. He called out: "All aboard; all aboard." The train lurched forward to continue its southward journey.

Once in the Negro car, Roo reached back and closed the curtain near the inter-car door. He had hoped to soon see Vickie again. Roo reached under his seat and pulled his journal out. He opened the journal and started where he left off when he saw Vickie outside the train on the platform. He wrote:

> Well, I feel that I have reached a point of no return. I have taken a path of great resistance and hope that I will not pay greatly in the end. In my heart, I believe the reward will be very much worth the risk. Victoria Herd has become dear to me. She is becoming very much worth the battle I will most surely face ahead. Never did I believe that this would be a part of my manhood journey. What joy this woman brings me; what pain our relationship has in store...

Roo stopped in the middle of his entry and thought. Who will I share this with first? Dad? Mom? No it would have to be April. April has a level head. Nothing shakes her. She could bear the news of the White girl's interactions with him. Roo believed that April could also tolerate the knowledge of knowing that Vickie was a White Tulsan: whose citizens were responsible for the destruction of the Greenwood District — the home of Uncle Benjamin, their relatives, and friends. Yes, April could bear it. She wouldn't jump to conclusions. She would be the perfect ally. She was smart and well spoken. Indeed, men know how to strategize when given the potential for battle. Of course, Roo realized that this would not be simply a battle with southern standards, i.e., appropriate racial interactions and relationships, but his family's battle to preserve his emotional and physical safety. Society would **push** him back, and his family would **pull** him back. Ummm, he would probably just have to go it alone...as a man.

Unbeknown to Roo and Vickie was the seven-year-old White boy with red hair, who was at that point trying to get his grandfather's attention back at the train station. The boy tugged at his grandfather's suspenders. His frustrated grandfather finally turned from the station's ticket agent to give his grandson the attention he pressed him for. "Grandpa, grandpa..." The elderly gentleman removed his spectacles and stared down at the boy. The boy had to stop to catch his breath. "Grandpa, I just saw a White girl kiss a 'niggra.' They were just dancing over there." The boy pointed toward the front train entrance. The ticket agent stopped stamping the tickets and bowed his head down near the counter to hear the boy. The boy continued, "He had a hat on just like mine." He pointed to his brown flat-cap. The agent chimed in, "Sonny, what did the White girl look like?" "She was 'petty' — like Dena," the boy responded. The grandfather interjected: Dena is his cousin." "Well, do you mean pretty?" The agent asked. "Uh huh," the boy said while nodding his head. "She 'come' in and walked out there..." he pointed to the station platform doors. The agent quickly excused himself, and rushed over to the station platform doors. As he already knew, the train was long gone. "I've been bamboozled," he muttered with an Irish accent. The agent rushed back to call ahead to the next train station. As the boy and his grandfather watched, the agent picked up the desk phone and said to the switchboard operator: "Emma, connect me to 'Charlie – 533.' " The ticket agent's jaw tightened and then dropped. He hung up the phone and dropped his head in a defeated pose. The boy's grandfather asked, "What happened mister?" Without lifting his head to face the boy's grandfather, he responded, "The phone wires are down, they won't be live until tomorrow around supper..." The ticket agent then abruptly lifted his head and pointed his right index finger up above his head and exclaimed: "We'll stop the shenanigans yet..." He turned his head toward a corner office and called out: "Rueben, Rueben; get the station truck and take a run to the next station and try to catch up with train 333; oooh," the agent stopped in mid-statement. He rubbed his bald head and spoke out loud again, "The downed line is blocking the highway: Rueben would never catch them using the country road..." Roo had unknowingly dodged, yet, another bullet.

Roo's anger and frustration with White people was now tempered by his wonderful and dynamic relationship with the beautiful White girl, Vickie — a "representative" of the Tulsa Whites that had engaged in battle with Greenwood residents... indeed, a relationship made the difference. Vickie, perhaps, would not receive the same understanding and mercy with those along her future path: those who would discover that she came from the city that decimated a community. Before his mind drifted from the thought, he considered the question: "Am I a traitor?"

In his "mind's ears," Roo could "hear" the music that he and Vickie danced to in the shadows of the train station, now a hundred and thirteen miles behind them. He was reliving the moment: the closeness of their beings, the smell of her hair, the depth of her blue eyes, the taste of her lips. As he began to feel the heaviness of his eye lids, reality gradually merged into fantasy. He was now in the middle of a "dream-embellished" spin with Vickie — lifting her light and delicate body from the ground; high enough to press his cheek against her breast — they "were" salient; firm against his face. The tips of his fingers were "ultra-sensitive." He could feel the soft and tender quality of her flesh through the material of her sheer and delicate dress about her waist and hips...The scent of black licorice, *NO*, peppermint was in the air. He gently and slowly lowered her; allowing her body to drag against his. The front of her bright colored dress began to be pulled upward as he allowed her body to move downward. The hem of her dress was at her knees, now just above her knee caps; the band of her flesh-colored stockings were exposed — now her mid-thighs — her legs were long, toned and taut...***he held the power***... the hem of Vickie's dress moved still higher exposing the round curves of her...Roo dozed off into a peaceful sleep...

CHAPTER TWELVE

"The Eerie Dream — Part Two"

1964 - The Professor

When Randolph came to himself, he realized that he had an audience. The attention was on him. His person — his presence — was the focus of the setting... He was standing before his college, summer-semester history class: in the middle of a lecture. His students were all wide-eyed as they stared at Randolph Jefferson Author, their unusually quiet and somber history professor...The word was out. As he pondered and then spoke, his audience began to grow as professors and students from other classes quietly entered his lecture room and lined the walls. Professor Author was considered well-versed in his knowledge and very charismatic in his presentation. Randolph had considered that his affinity for dates and events came from his mother and, perhaps, a portion of his presentation style came as the result of his admiration and observations of his great train-riding mentor... Dr. Robert Jones, M.D. Today, this history lecture was different; special — Dr. Author had lived it.

A student, not yet aware of Dr. Author's personal experience of the Tulsa Riots, asked the question: "Professor, reports of the Tulsa Riots indicate that 50 to 300 people died. Why is there such a large range? Which would you say is most accurate?" Dr. Author, with a hint of introspection, responded: "Some died instantly — on the spot; others died subsequently, as a result of their wounds and injuries — and some died emotionally on that day — the latter, of course, have never and will never have their sort of death reported... they will never be in the count. Indeed, there have been many years of grieving — rather than counting." Dr. Author continued: "The cessation of life, for many, also represented the death of ambition, drive, and healthy goals. Of course, there are those factors that linger that one hopes would die; that is, the memory of the prejudice, hatred, and violence." His usually projective and authoritative voice trailed off to a whisper. Dr. Author stood silent; transfixed. The young students observed Professor Author's face as it appeared to age before their eyes. They noticed a single tear slide down his cheek...

The one casualty Randolph had tried to block from his mind was that of the wise and eloquent, Dr. Robert Jones... Randolph, standing in front of his students, was reflecting and processing a huge amount of information as well as sorting through his emotions as he now, recounted the scene and vision of the good, Dr. Jones. He hadn't often allowed himself to direct his mind on these thoughts — even when he was on the train back to Georgia: no, nothing except for that **odd vision**. But here, 1964; forty-three years after the riots, in this magnificent institution of higher learning for Black young men, in Atlanta, Georgia, he allowed his mind to drift... and yes, he felt he owed it to his students, at this moment, to **think out loud** — to hear the mental processes of a historian.

"Yes, young men, history...my recount. I can remember running down the street, Greenwood Avenue, as fast as my legs could carry me. My relatives and I moved hurriedly through the once busy intersections." As he painted the gruesome and grotesque picture of a district in turmoil: the debris, burnt out automobiles, damaged store fronts, screams and the wounded, he wiped a salient tear from his cheek. The sight of their professor was moving. Everyone in the class sat and stood still. It was a solemn moment. He paused and scanned the classroom, seemingly looking in the eyes of everyone present. "I can recall looking back, at one point, as I moved with my group... I tripped over debris — broken toys, bottles, bricks — while holding onto my cousin's shoulder — we held up the rear with the women and children ahead of us. Dr. Robert Jones, M.D., yes; I can see his face in my mind's eye." Professor Author walked across the room and looked out the window. He continued, "He was a prominent physician in the community. Dr. Jones was on his knees attending to a small girl who was trapped under a large collapsed sign and bricks... He urged us to move on and leave him with the young girl. As I looked back at the physician with great fear in my heart, I saw my friend die... the voice of a great, wise and profoundly influential character was stilled." A few of the young students picked up their pencils and began writing. The rest looked bewildered, befuddled - troubled.

During Professor Author's stimulating lecture, an announcement was made on a television broadcast and shared classroom to classroom by a student-messenger. The young, student-messenger quietly stepped in the classroom, caught Professor Author's attention, and when granted permission — as a result of the professor's head nod; announced, "Professors, fellow students; The Civil Rights Act has been signed by Lyndon Johnson, President of our United States of America..." The standing-room-only crowd erupted in a cheer and long applause — many standing along the walls started hugging one another. After the announcement, Professor Author promptly stated, "My grandfather was alive to witness the **Civil War,** I count myself blessed to be alive to witness the **Civil Rights Act.**" The stream of tears began to flow... most noticeably, on the faces of the Negro professors. Many of them had participated and been a part of the process...

Professor Author finished his lecture; his account of the events of June 1st, 1921, in Tulsa, Oklahoma to a rousing applause from his audience: his colleagues and students. He finished his presentation where his Uncle Ben had finished with his magnificent and moving words of encouragement to him 43 years earlier on the Negro car of his home-bound train: **"community"** and **"carpenters."** Many approached him at the front of the class to shake his hand and offer brief comments and accolades. Many others began to file out to quickly head to the student center to hear more on the Civil Rights 'Bill' signing. Professor Author had also planned to rush over to the center to hear more on the event once he collected his belongings.

Professor Randolph Jefferson Author was now en route to the student center to join in on the jubilation and celebration — the civil rights document had finally reached the President of the United States of America, the highest desk in the country; and, its principles would finally seep to the lowest reaches of the socially impoverished and marginalized... He thought about his life; his story within the story of the civil rights process. He considered that he was now a man of 60 years of age. Many who had left an indelible impression on his life were now resting in their graves — finally relieved of their toils and hard labor: his grandfather, John; Uncle Benjamin; Aunt Beth; other uncles, aunts and relatives — he lost a few cousins in the second world war. And yes, friends, such as Mr. Smithson were also departed — he had lived to be 102 years old. He was grateful that his parents, Rachel and Joseph, were both alive and very active in their community: they were both in their eighties. His sister April was the founder and operator of her own beauty college — was there any doubt that this would come to fruition? And his numerous cousins were functioning very well in their own right. Michael Author had helped rebuild Author Financial and was doing very well for himself and his family: he and Jo Ann had 10 children. They had married one year, to-the-date, of the riot in order to have a positive and triumphant memory to rival the historic and tragic event. Randolph now had a wonderful wife, Catherine, who he had met during college and married while he was in graduate school. They had four children: two boys and two girls. They had a large house near the campus. He had spent many hours sharing his story with his children... William, Rosaline, Carolyn, and Joseph; the youngest named for his father. True to his mother's statement, he found that his story helped build their lives and personal stories. Professor Author frequently referenced his aged and scarred journal: the one his mother gave him in 1921 as a travel gift — he kept it in the original gift box with the now faded, long bow. He had shared his life experiences with them line by line; page by page. At points when his entries had seemed a bit too risqué or inappropriate for the children, rather than quote the entry, he paraphrased and embellished. He always made sure they walked away knowing the general theme he had attempted to share with them.

Dr. Author considered that a lot of time had passed since the riots of 1921; but not the memories. He thought: they must not pass from our conscious and conscience — they mustn't be loss. Professor Author lamented the fact that he didn't get the chance to fully **know** Vickie. There was still a deep level of intimacy that he had wished to share with her. It was a level beyond the physical: it was the spiritual; the psychological he was after. Although he realized that much of his experience of her had been physical and emotional; he concluded that many females shared these alluring qualities. But he had wanted to know what made Vickie, the White girl, tick. What made her such a *treasure* to White men? What was it like to navigate through life with social privileges? Did she have the same wants and desires as the Negro girls he knew? How did she truly see him? He wanted to get inside her mind. He wanted to tap into her worldview. He wanted to touch, explore, "experiment," and "dissect"... But, it wasn't to be. Although they had planned to stay in touch and eventually get together; they found that the ways and attitudes of the 1920's South was a barrier that was virtually impenetrable when it came to inter-racial, romantic relationships. Randolph Author often thought: One is more likely to witness the mixing of oil with the running waters of the Mississippi River than an inter-racial relationship between a Negro man and White woman — in the heart of Dixie...

Following the celebratory activities on campus, Professor Author walked over to his parked car: a beige, 1964, Chevrolet Impala coupe. He bought the car following Joseph's departure to college. He paused and thought — all is well... The now, senior fellow sat in his new vehicle and started it. Professor Author put his automatic vehicle into gear and headed off campus en route to his nearby house. A few blocks from campus he noticed another vehicle that looked exactly like his, parked on the side with its flashers on. Professor Author was intrigued at the sight of the other car; to the point of slowing down to take a closer look — he had to compare his vehicle with the vehicle parked to the side. He thought; ah, it's a coupe like mine: yes, same side mirrors. Wow, even the interior looks like mine. When he came to the front of the parked Impala, he noticed a sight that was awe-striking. Leaning back against the grill of the car was a young, White woman with long, blonde hair. She had a gas can sitting at her feet. She turned her head and gazed at the vehicle; amazed at its similarity to her car and then looked at the driver and smiled. Professor Author was mesmerized — it was Victoria Herd — same bright smile, rosy-cheeked dimples, long hair, and deep blue eyes. She was beautiful in every way. Of course, it wasn't Vickie; it couldn't be Vickie. Victoria Herd had to be 60 years old... but she looked every bit like his friend of old. He stopped the car to see if he could be of assistance. She carefully lifted herself to a standing position, grimacing when she touched the corner of the hot hood that had been exposed to the blazing sun with her hand. Professor Author noticed the radiant heat emanating from it. She approached the Professor's passenger side window and bent over to address him. "Hello, sir...my name is Jenny, short for Jennifer." Her long, golden blonde hair fell over her shoulders. The front of her white sun dress drooped open, exposing her white bra. Professor Author tried to discretely advert his eyes — casually looking over her shoulder at her car behind her, and then back to her face. She continued, "I'm out of gas..." Past her hanging top, portions of her flat belly and round navel were visible to the professor as she occasionally lifted her head as though looking over the roof of his car across the street: did she do this on purpose — he thought... he was aroused. He was embarrassed.

Hopefully, she couldn't tell... at once, his eyes fell on the up and down movement of her partially exposed stomach as she spoke... an elastic band in the waist of the dress prevented him from seeing more. She again looked down at the professor and spontaneously began to giggle. He noticed that her stomach tensed as she laughed. Why is she laughing, he thought. Professor Author, taking into account the social climate of the 1964 South, asked, "Can I help you by getting some gas in your gas can and..." Before he could finish his question — ("...and bring it back?") — the White woman opened his passenger door and sat in the seat placing the gas can on the floor near her white sneakers. "Thank you, sir," she said instantly. The professor cleared his throat and said, "Uh, you're welcome." He directed his vehicle toward the nearest filling station, two-miles away. "Jennifer," he asked, "why were you standing outside in the heat?" She responded, "I was tired of sitting in the car. The car was shaded by the trees when I finally decided to get out. I realized that while I sat in the car, no one could tell that I needed help — that was another reason to get out." Professor Randolph responded, "I see... my name is Dr. Author, I'm a professor at the college; a couple of blocks from where your car is parked." The young White woman looked at the professor and smiled. She said, "Nice to meet you professor. Oh, that's not my car; the car belongs to my Uncle Bruce and Aunt Meg. I'm visiting from Tulsa, Oklahoma. I'm on college break." The professor's eyebrows lifted at the mention of Tulsa. "I see," he said. He stated before thinking: "You look amazingly like a friend I knew in Tulsa." The White woman asked, "What's her name?" "Her last name is Herd..." She responded, excitedly, "I know the Herd family... they're a family of doctors — the son was my doctor for a few years. He once told me something that I thought was funny." Professor Author briefly took his eyes off the road to look at her. "He said that his family use to call him 'Rascal' when he was growing up." Randolph thought:

that's incredible; this woman is talking about Vickie's brother Terrance... He chuckled on the inside and thought: he's a doctor?

The young, red-headed filling station attendant pumped the gas into the gas can, while smoking a long cigarette — he kept peering at the pretty White woman in the front seat. Professor Author got out and paid for the gas while the young college-aged woman waited comfortably in the new Impala. When the attendant finished, Professor Author placed the full gas can in the trunk and then walked to the front of the filling station. The professor briefly disappeared from the young woman's sight. A minute later, he returned with two soda pops and handed one to the young woman waiting in the car. An older White filling station attendant watched from the gas station window. He gave the two a good, long, hard stare; smirked and then turned back to his evening newspaper. The red-headed attendant spit twice on the windshield and smeared it with a red rag he pulled out of his back pocket. The professor grimaced at the sight, started the car, and drove off; with his windshield wipers in the high position...

Jennifer, after delicately biting down on the corner of her bottom lip, and running her fingers through her hair, smiled and placed her hand on top of Professor Author's hand — resting on the bench seat between them — and said, "Professor, thank you kindly." She paused and finished, "I'm in your debt." He nodded his head in silence. Here, in the Year of Our Lord, 1964, Randolph was 60 years old; a prominent college professor, the husband of an adorable and solid wife, and father of four marvelous adult children. His passenger was a college-aged, beautiful, White, co-ed with the deepest blue eyes: he felt that he was riding with his dear friend Vickie. Like Vickie, in that downtown Tulsa hide-a-way across from "Puddintangs," his current passenger seemed very relaxed in his presence. She took the liberty of pulling the hem of her dress, which was near her knees, up to her mid-thigh — exposing her firm and shapely legs. She began rapidly waving her right hand in front of her face as though simulating the movement of a hand-fan. She moved her legs back and forth — at times bumping her knees together. He could hear the slapping sound of her flesh. She exclaimed, "Boy is it hot..." The professor was transfixed. Jennifer was so "Vickie-like."

After establishing some level of comfort from the heat, Jennifer asked, "Professor, can I turn on your radio?" Without looking toward her, Professor Author managed a slight smile and head nod. Jennifer stopped fanning, reached toward the knobs of Professor Author's radio, and turned it on — full blast... Motown great Mary Wells was singing "My Guy..." Jennifer began slapping her exposed legs with her hands as though playing a set of bongos; she was off beat. The professor could see the red imprints that her hands left on her white legs after each slap. She closed her eyes and continued slapping her thighs. Her dress inched up to her upper thighs as she occasionally lifted one leg, then the other. "Man, I love this song..." she said; seeming oblivious to the movement of her dress and the world around her. Jennifer sang out the words: "MY GUY..." as the professor blurted out: "Oh, my..." He noticed that he was, now, tightly clinching the steering wheel as though hanging on for dear life...

The loud and soulful tune sounded just in time to catch the attention of an elderly Black woman sitting at a nearby bus stop. The woman looked over the rims of her cat-shaped glasses at the professor and his White female passenger as his car paused at the stop sign. The Black woman sighed, tightened her lips and then turned to rummage through a grocery bag sitting on the bench beside her. The professor pressed the accelerator and proceeded across the intersection before he heard the sound of a police siren directly behind him. He nervously looked in his rearview mirror and noticed two policemen looking at his car... Whoa, he thought; it was Bill Jackson and Johnny Wheeler; two of Atlanta's Black policemen. They both knew the professor and acknowledged him with their siren and a wave. All was well...

They returned to the young White woman's car without incident. While they had passed many Whites, and Negroes for that matter, en route to the filling station and back, no one went out of their way to cause a problem. Amen, Professor Author thought. The White woman with the long blonde locks slowly and casually exited the professor's car. Professor Author got out of the Impala and walked to the trunk to retrieve her gas can. She stood close to him and waited for him to relay the can to her, but he closed the trunk and walked past her to the gas-door of her car — he knew exactly were it was; they had identical cars... She smiled and followed. He emptied the contents of the gas can into her vehicle's gas tank without a word — he simply looked at her and smiled. At 60, Professor Author still had a bright, faultless smile — however, it was now ringed by a gray goatee. At this stage in his life, the professor was considered to be not only handsome, but now, a distinguished and debonair gentlemen. He often turned heads as he walked past the ladies, with his stately posture. He took pride in, according to some, appearing 15 years younger than his contemporaries... The young, White woman leaned against her uncle's car and watched as the Professor removed the nozzle from the tank's orifice. Professor Author placed the gas can in the trunk of the young woman's vehicle, closed the trunk, and rubbed his hands together exclaiming:

"All done..." Before he knew it, the young woman bounded toward him and embraced him, and kissed him on his left cheek. In her nearness, and over the potent, and nearly asphyxiating, gas fumes, he could tell that she smelled like flowers. He could feel the movement of her chest against his body as she breathed in and out. Still holding him, she looked up at his face with an intense stare — as though studying him. At this moment, the professor felt powerless, snared by her inescapable blue eyes. The young, White co-ed, at this moment, had the power. She released him and stepped back just before an oncoming car full of what appeared to be Black college students reached them: but not before reaching over to squeeze his left bicep. She said, displaying Vickie-like dimples, "You have very firm muscles... Sir, I'm in your debt."

With a quickness that seemed to be in direct contrast to her slow and casual movement up to that point, she jumped in her uncle's car, started the engine, and pulled off. She saluted the professor with three short chirps on the horn: beep-beep-beep... Jennifer waved her long, toned arm out the window before disappearing around the corner. Professor Author walked around and stood in front of his Impala with his left hand covering his mouth. He reached in the jacket pocket with his other hand and pulled out a smoking pipe. Taking his time, he pulled out a pouch of tobacco and set up his pipe. His mind, now a quandary of thoughts, again fell on his friend, Vickie: thoughts resurrected by his recent interaction with the beautiful, young co-ed. He was piecing things together with regard to the issue of relationships as he held his unlit pipe. He realized that the presumptions one person has about another limits their desire to explore and learn more about that person. When it came to White-Black interactions, it seemed that Whites thought they knew all there was to Blacks; and Blacks thought they knew all they needed to know about

Whites: and that's that... but Randolph realized that a true and bountiful relationship began by limiting ones presumptions and engaging a desire to learn and discover facets of *the unknown other*... He considered the story in the Bible about the friendship of David and Jonathan, the son of the first Israelite King, Saul. He remembered his childhood Sunday school teacher talk about the depth of their relationship — to the point of Jonathan siding with his dear friend, David, over his father, Saul... it seemed that their very souls were connected — "the soul of Jonathan was knitted with the soul of David, and Jonathan loved him as his own soul." He believed that this was the level of relationship he was forming with Vickie... that, beyond race.

Alas, what had started with an unsettling dream in his parents' home in 1921 had followed him; or maybe led him through, the valleys of turmoil and pain; the peaks of wisdom and conscientiousness; the face of friend and foe; and to this — a place of reckoning... a place that his great, great grandfather Mazumba; grandfather, John; Uncle Benjamin; Dr. Jones and the Black men who gave all to protect their woman and family: including those in the great Greenwood District, would marvel to see... a place and period of *civil "rights"* rather than *civil "war"*, a period of integration rather than segregation; a period of seeing a White woman ride in a car with a Black man without incident.

Still looking at the corner the young White woman had turned, the professor lit the pipe, thinking on the events of the past 45 minutes, and then back to a comment made by his friend Vickie, four decades earlier, and 700 hundreds miles from his current position: Maybe we're closer to the *"moon"* than I realized...

JEFFREY A. POUNCEY

REFERENCES

1. "Atlantic Coast Line Railroads." *Wikipedia*. 11
   June 2009. 11 June 2009.
   <http://en.wikipedia.org/wiki/
   Atlantic_Coast_Line_Railroad>.

2. "Spelman College." *Wikipedia*. 25 Dec. 2009.
   25 Dec. 2009. <http://en.wikipedia.org/
   wiki/Spelman_College>.

3. "John D. Rockefeller." *Wikipedia*. 7 Aug. 2009.
   7 Aug. 2009. <http://en.wikipedia.org/wiki/
   John_D._Rockefeller>.

4. Women in History. Madame C. J. Walker
   biography. Last Updated: 7/29/2010. Lakewood
   Public Library. Date accessed 6/21/2010 .
   <http://www.lkwdpl.org/wihohio/walk-
   mad.htm>.

5.   Handy, W.C. "St. Louis Blue." 1914.

6.   Green, Eddie. "A Good Man Is Hard To Find."
     1919.

7.   Johnson, H. (2007) The Oklahoma Historical
     Society's Encyclopedia of Oklahoma History &
     Culture.

8. "Greenwood, Tulsa, Oklahoma." *Wikipedia*. 3
     June
     2009.http://en.wikipedia.org/wiki/Greenwood,
     _Tulsa,_Oklahoma.

9.   Johnson, H. (2007) The Oklahoma Historical

     Society's Encyclopedia of Oklahoma History &

     Culture.

10. Ibid.

11. "The Birth of a Nation Synopsis." *Fandango*. 2009 <http://www.fandango.com/thebirthofanation v5751/summary>.

12. "Birth of a Nation." *TCM*. 16 Oct. 2009. http://www.tcm.com/mediaroom/index.jsp?cid=1 34463.

13. 14th Census of the United States taken in the Year 1920 Vol. III Population 1920.

14. Wallace, R., "Black Wallstreet: A Lost Dream." *e-line productions*.http://www.deveyd.com/blackwallp olitic.html.

15. Berlin, Irvin. "God Bless America." 1918.

16. "Black Wallstreet." *eLine Productions*.

    http://www.daveyd.com/index.html 2009.

17. "The Cactus Kid." *Wikipedia*. May 30, 2009.

    http://en.wikipedia.org/wiki/The_Cactus_Kid.

18. "Buildings of Tulsa, Oklahoma." *Wikipedia*. 28

    Sept. 2008. 28 Sept. 2008.

    <http://en.wikipedia.org/wiki/

    Buildings_of_Tulsa,_Oklahoma>.

19. "Tulsa County Medical Society" - A History of

    Tulsa Hospitals 1900-1968.

20. The King James Version. Donald C. Stamps, ed.

    Grand Rapids: Zondervan Publishing House.

    1992.

21. Carlson, Marc, I. *The Tulsa Race Riot of 1921* - Timeline of the Tulsa Race Riot." Copyright © 2001. http://www.personal.utulsa.edu/~Marc-Carlson/riot/tulsatime.html.

22. Ibid.

23. Ibid.

24. Ibid.

25. Ibid.

26. Ibid.

27. Ibid.

28. Ibid.

29. Ibid.

30. Ibid.

31. Ibid.

32. Ibid.

33. Ibid.

34. Ibid.

35. Ibid.

36. Ibid.

37. Ibid.

38. Ibid.

39. Ibid.

40. Ibid.

41. *Nectar and Ambrosia: An Encyclopedia of Food*

    in World Mythology, Tamra

    Andrews [ABC-CLIO: Santa Barbara] 2000 (p.151)

42. Smokey Robinson, My Guy, March 13, 1964.

    Hitsville, USA.

A

A.D. 1964

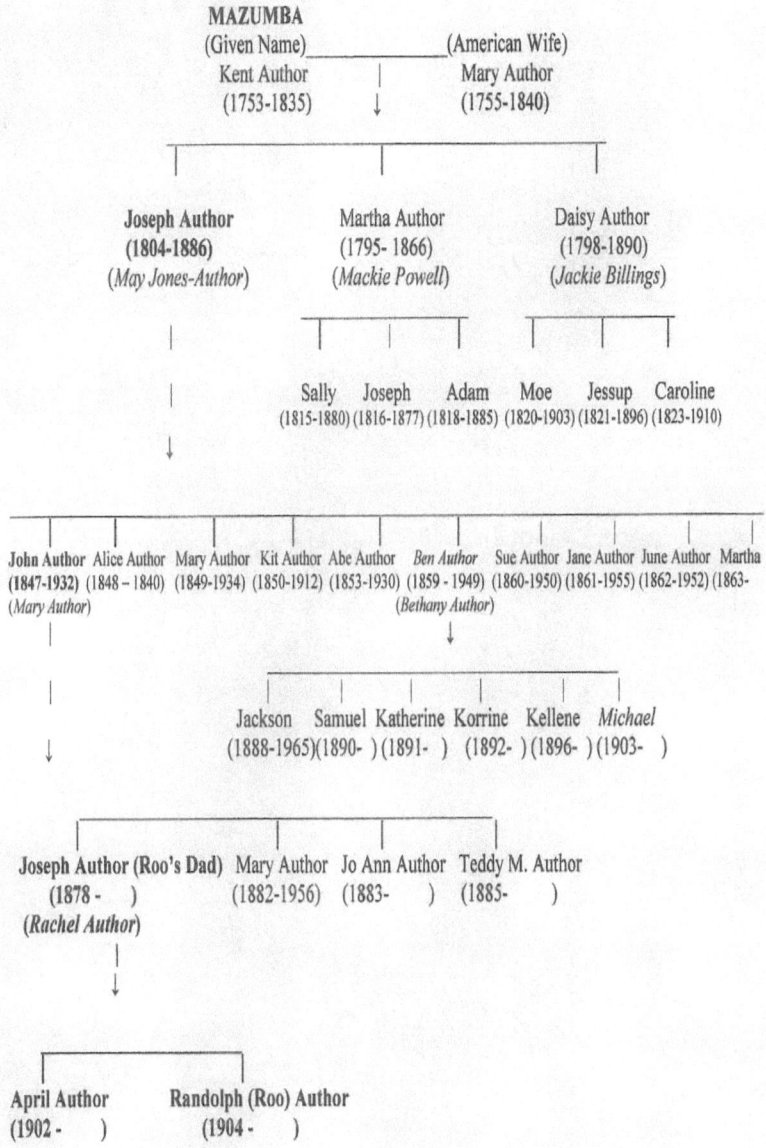

MAZUMBA
(Given Name)_____(American Wife)
Kent Author | Mary Author
(1753-1835) ↓ (1755-1840)

Joseph Author	Martha Author	Daisy Author
(1804-1886)	(1795- 1866)	(1798-1890)
(*May Jones-Author*)	(*Mackie Powell*)	(*Jackie Billings*)

Sally   Joseph   Adam   Moe   Jessup   Caroline
(1815-1880) (1816-1877) (1818-1885) (1820-1903) (1821-1896) (1823-1910)

John Author Alice Author Mary Author Kit Author Abe Author *Ben Author* Sue Author Jane Author June Author Martha
(1847-1932) (1848 – 1840) (1849-1934) (1850-1912) (1853-1930) (1859 - 1949) (1860-1950) (1861-1955) (1862-1952) (1863-
(*Mary Author*) (*Bethany Author*)

Jackson   Samuel   Katherine   Korrine   Kellene   *Michael*
(1888-1965)(1890-) (1891-) (1892-) (1896-)(1903-   )

Joseph Author (Roo's Dad) Mary Author Jo Ann Author Teddy M. Author
(1878 -   ) (1882-1956) (1883-   ) (1885-   )
(*Rachel Author*)

April Author **Randolph (Roo) Author**
(1902 -   ) (1904 -   )

JEFFREY A. POUNCEY

ABOUT THE AUTHOR

Dr. Jeff Pouncey, a clinically trained child neuropsychologist, believes that no medium is out of bounds when conveying one's history, heritage, identity, and self-awareness; hence, the historical fiction story — Midnight Tear. Dr. Pouncey's training in psychology and the neurosciences with children and adults, as well as society's "elders" in skilled nursing hospitals, has prompted him to realize that one's life experiences and social identity are not locked in the stages of growth and development, but the experiences that bridge the *transition* between the stages. Dr. Pouncey seizes every opportunity to bring awareness to the connection of one's social, economic, and emotional well-being to their mental well-being: especially, when society intrudes on that sense of well-being.

In addition to Midnight Tear, Dr. Pouncey writes children's stories, non-fiction, social and scientific essays, and has completed a well-received research-dissertation study: "Acute Effects of Anesthesia on Attention in Pediatric Patients." He is the co-owner and operator of a consulting business and teaches undergraduate behavioral health and neuroscience classes.

Dr. Pouncey resides in the "state" of "Excitement for gaining and sharing knowledge and information," has been married to Brunetta for 19 years, and has three children: Xavier, Jenesis and Joel.